Here There Be Lawyers

Here There Be Lawyers

David Gerrold

Star Traveler Press

ISBN-13: 979-8-9925058-3-2 (paperback)
ISBN-13: 979-8-9925058-4-9 (eBook)

Here There Be Lawyers copyright © 2025 by David Gerrold

Editor and Publisher: Justin T. O'Conor Sloane
Cover art: *Caution!* © 2025 by David Gerrold
Book design by Katerina Bruno

Published by Star Traveler Press
an imprint of Starship Sloane Publishing Company, Inc.
Austin-Round Rock, Texas, USA

starshipsloane.com

Printed in the United States of America & internationally

CONTENTS

INSIGHT

T he first mistake was law school.
Everything after that was consequences.

LUNA

The defendants were a married couple, married quite recently. In fact, they were still on their honeymoon.

Good-looking pair. Sexy red-headed lady and a tall black man with a Scottish name. They were both middle-aged, but well-preserved and terribly well mannered—and unfortunately just wealthy enough to think that they were somehow exempt from the laws of the universe. Seems they'd 'adopted' a street orphan on Luna, then felt betrayed when he'd acted exactly like a street orphan.

Truth was, they'd railroaded the kid into an adoption, practically blackmailed the poor jerk—caught him on a purse-snatch, but instead of turning him in to the local constabulary, did a fast flim-flammery with a lot of legal-sounding doubletalk and convinced the idiot that he had no rights because he wasn't a taxpayer, therefore they had the right to kill him unless he learned some manners pretty damn quick. They promised to teach him manners. Some joke. When was the last time anyone learned manners from blackmailers?

What they did instead was use the kid as a slave. They made him carry their luggage. Instead of wages, they gave him the benefit of their infinite wisdom. "Hothouse wisdom," actually. A delicate bouquet of ideas, very pretty in a rigidly controlled environment, but not practical at all in the real world. The irony is that they brought him to Turtledome, one of the most rigidly controlled environments this side of Clavius. All that stands between us and vacuum is a triple-hull of polycarbon weave and a meter of magnetized water for shielding.

Of course none of their high-mounted philosophizing made much sense to the kid. They'd never missed a meal. He'd been sleeping in steam vents. They lectured him incessantly on manners and responsibility and his lack thereof —they repeatedly embarrassed him in public— and then they were astonished that he didn't feel any loyalty to them. And after all they'd done for him. Really, how stupid can you get? You don't even train a puppy that way—why should it work on a human being?

I guess they thought they were being benevolent—but you don't sit a starving chimpanzee down at a banquet table and then punish him because he doesn't know which fork

3

to use. This poor idiot wasn't even capable of being responsible for himself, he was a street orphan! How could he be responsible to a family he hadn't even chosen, for god's sake, but had been blackmailed into? The poor kid was still operating at the level of hunger! They hadn't even given him a hug and they expected manners and loyal devotion? Stupid, stupid!

Oh. My decision?

I put the kid into the empathy corps where he had a chance of learning some self-respect—that being the primary prerequisite to responsibility. And the dome would get some useful work out of him, cleaning up after tourists. Then I fined the would-be "parents" for keeping an unlicensed slave and sent them to Coventry.

Well, I couldn't very well let them run around loose, could I? They had a bizarre sense of participation. Something about how if a community doesn't meet the individual's beliefs about how it should be run, then the individual has the right to disregard its authority. (Well, yes, rebellion in the face of injustice is justified, I wrote that essay in high school, but ever since they handed me a gavel, I don't have a lot of patience for those who disrespect the authority of the court. And let me add this, despite my refusal to run, I was elected anyway.)

I guess that kind of stuff sounded real good when they preached it to each other in the privacy of their own bedroom, but it sure caused a lot of havoc to the people around them. I don't think they'll learn manners in Coventry, but they might learn something about cooperation.

And even if not, at least it'll keep them out of trouble for a couple years.

It wasn't a bad ruling. Grandpa upheld it.

ARBITERS

I'm an arbiter.

There aren't enough cases here to justify the expense of a full-time senior. Maybe in Clavius or Tycho City, but not here in Turtledome. Even Grandpa is only part time. The rest of us take turns, working the misdemeanors and Grandpa reviews everything, whether it's appealed or not.

Once a week, he holds review. If there are no cases, he pits us against each other, tossing out hypothetical situations so we can argue the law. It keeps us on our toes.

Sometimes he takes a side and argues against us. If we can win the argument—which doesn't happen often, sometimes he has a thumb on the scale—we get to sit on a higher-level case.

It's not a reward. It's a consequence.

THE IDIOT

The tourist was an idiot.

His second mistake was resisting the Monitor.

The tourist was also twenty-three kilos over standard, and that did not exactly endear him to us either. Mass is a luxury. Only the wealthy can afford that much.

I inherited the whole mess because, despite the end of the trimester, my replacement was out pregnant, so I was still serving as an arbiter.

You could read the whole thing from the transcript, I suppose, but I'll save you the trouble. Sis was almost fourteen, but she was small for her age and skinny too, so the groundhog took her for a child.

It was midpoint of second shift on the Promenade, main arcade, and the idiot dropped an ice cream wrapper on the slidewalk while staring blatantly past the Monitor.

Jennifer—nickname Spinning Jenny, for her maneuvers in low-grav dance—was polite about it. Rule One: be polite to the tourists. They're paying for it. Although, personally, I've always felt it would be a hell of a lot less trouble if they would just send us their money and we could mail them their souvenirs, moon rocks and nausea. She asked the litterbeast to please pick up his wrapper.

The groundhog replied, and I quote, "Piss off, kid."

Jenny realized immediately that she was talking to a cultural illiterate. It happens occasionally that someone arrives at Turtledome having skipped the orientation. Usually, it's someone who's so rich and abusive that there aren't a lot of people around to say, "Sit down, shut your cock hole, and listen up. Your life might depend on this."

Jenny flashed her shield at the man and explained to him that she was a Monitor and she was requesting him to please be responsible for cleaning up after himself.

According to the witnesses, the man looked annoyed for only the briefest of instants, then turned his back on Jenny and continued his conversation with his partner. Jenny then stepped in front of him and repeated her request. "If you do not comply, I will be forced to place you under arrest. This is your only warning."

The idiot backhanded her into the

slidewalk railing with a growl, "Get away from me, you little bleeder."

Jenny didn't even have to punch her trouble-beeper. She did, of course—she did everything right by the rule book, but it was actually irrelevant. Two MT's and the ice cream seller pinned the man to the wall first.

By the time Jenny had finished standing up and wiping the blood from her nose, there was a sizable crowd forming. To give Jenny credit, she told them to disperse, asking for assistance only from the two MT's and the ice cream seller. She turned to the tourist and began to read him his rights and a list of charges.

"You are charged with littering, resisting the Monitor, striking a Monitor, disorderly conduct—" The tape has a muffled protest from the groundhog that is not quite translatable at this point, but Jenny heard it clear enough. "—verbal abuse, and resisting arrest. I advise you to shut up now before you make matters worse for yourself. You have the right to remain silent, and in this case, it's probably a good idea. You have the right to an attorney. If you do not have one, you're an idiot. This entire transaction is being recorded and the recording will be used as evidence in a court of law. You have the right to —" Etc. It's all on the public record.

And I inherited the whole mess because it was my trimester to serve as *pro tempore* defender of the public interests. That meant I had to find some way to prepare a defense. To make it worse, Grandpa would hear the case.

Arraignment was scheduled for first hour, third shift. We don't like wasting time in the dome. Oxygen-suckers use up resources. Even though they do end up paying for their incarceration, we still have to wait for payment until sentence is passed.

I sat with the man for forty-five minutes. The first twenty minutes was listening to him complain about the unfairness of it all. Finally, I interrupted. "You're paying for my time. And I am not cheap."

Amazingly, he shut.

"You're a guest here, not a citizen. That gives you certain privileges that citizens do not enjoy. But insulting the local government is not one of them. For that, you have to pay taxes. Now, I've reviewed the charges—" I stopped. "I'm required to tell you that I do have a conflict of interest in this case. The Monitor is my little sister. And yes, she is a brat, but she's still a Monitor. If you wish, you can ask for a different arbiter. But unless you can afford it, it wouldn't be a good idea—because there are no other arbiters available, and it would take at least a week, probably longer, to find another certified advocate on Luna willing to take your case, and whether or not they'd be available is problematic. They'd have to interrupt their own schedules to come to Turtledome. You probably couldn't afford that either. And no, they can't phone it in. We require personal appearance. So yes, you could ask for another, but it would take a lot of time and you would end up paying several fortunes of varying sizes, and while you waited you would be held without bail, so that would be another charge, if you're convicted, which you probably will be, and yes, I do agree, it isn't fair. I don't want to represent you either, but here we are, you're stuck with me and I'm stuck with you —"

I waited until he stopped to take a breath. "Yes, you're right. But that will not change the situation. Now, here's what I recommend. Plead no contest on the grounds of stupidity—yes, that is a legal option here—and the court will limit your fines to penalties, costs for time served, damages, emotional compensation, community service or a commensurate donation, and a public apology to the Monitor—"

Again I had to wait. "Let me remind you again, sir, that you are paying for my time and I am not cheap. If you want me to listen to your complaints, I will—but if you want me to represent you in court, we're running out of time. Yes, you can plead not guilty. That's always an option. The court will require a bond of a half million to cover the cost of your trial and associated expenses, such as continued incarceration, cost of your attorney, you may have an attorney of your own choosing, if you can find one on Luna willing to take your case, otherwise you'll have to bring one in from wherever, and of course, the ancillary expenses. It does add up. And yes, it's how we balance the budget. Now, if you can afford the half million—"

I glanced at my watch. Yes, I do wear one. It's an affectation, but it's a useful way to remind clients that they're paying for my time.

He shut up. Again. "Yes, I am listening to you. Yes, I am hearing what you're saying. And yes, I am here to represent you. I've given you my best advice. You're free to take it or not. If you wish, you can fire me. In fact, I hope you do. You'll still pay for the hour, of course, but you won't incur any further charges. But I really do not recommend representing yourself in Judge Ezra's courtroom. You'll find that Grandpa is not as sympathetic a listener as I am."

After a while, I continued, "Yes, he is my grandfather. He is also the Monitor's grandfather. That's in your favor. He knows she's a brat too. So he's likely to give you a little wiggle room. But there are witnesses who saw you strike her and—no, we do not accept bribes, if you want to buy your way out, I'm offering you the cheapest solution. That's the best I can do for you. In fact, it's the only thing I'm required to do for you."

I glanced at my watch again. We were now twenty minutes into the second hour. Another forty minutes and we'd be into overtime. I would have preferred to end this a lot sooner, but he wanted to rage and I was curious how long it would take him to run down and resign himself to the situation.

"Yes, I am required to defend you. That's what I'm doing here. But you have no case. You're guilty of breaking the law. The court has compelling evidence. There's no he-said/she-said here. The incident was recorded by three different cameras, plus the Monitor's own cam. There are no mitigating circumstances. You behaved like an asshole. There's no other story. And you're going to have to pay for being an asshole. That's how it works."

Yes, I was goading him. I was tired and I wanted him to just shut up and die. But he wouldn't and my policy is to let the accused rant as long as they want. It helps with the sentencing. But when he saw me studying my watch again, he stopped. "Yes, I am taking you serious. As serious as you can afford."

Apparently, that woke him up.

He asked how much.

I told him.

I showed him the whole menu. With taxes and fees, two hundred and fifty thousand. Three hundred without the apology. He cursed for a while, then agreed to the three hundred thou.

Grandpa accepted the plea with barely a grunt, although he did raise an eyebrow at my attached bill. "You let him talk, didn't you?"

I shrugged. "Gotta empty the cup before you can pour in more tea."

"Don't hand me that crap," Grandpa said. "I made it up." He initialed the form, passed it to the bailiff. Then he glared down at the tourist. "I don't care how rich you are, you're no longer welcome here. Book yourself on the next shuttle out. Mention my name, they'll make room. And one more thing, you're prohibited from returning to Turtledome—no, make that all Luna, for three years—"

"I object! I have important business here —"

"Okay, seven years." Grandpa scratched something on the paper. "I know what your business is. I've got your credit charges in front of me. Miss Sally won't miss you. She's got a waiting list. Goodbye, sir."

Then he turned to me. "My chambers—"

"Grandpa, I'm already on my second shift —"

"You can sleep in October."

"It is October—"

"Not now, it isn't. My chambers."

I followed him in. He wheeled around to face me. "I'm not going to argue with how you handled the case. I just want to point out that this will have repercussions. Public relations mostly, his friends, we're gonna lose that whole demographic."

"Yes, I'm well aware of that."

"I knew you would be. Did you do it deliberately?"

"Yes, sir."

"Okay. Good job."

PORTAL-
MASTER LOPEZ

Men with knobby knees should not wear short skirts.

Indeed, I'm not sure that men should wear skirts at all, but that may be a cultural bias. I was raised in Indiana, before the family immigrated to Luna.

I've often thought that anyone who wants to wear clothes that show off parts of their body should first have to pass an aesthetic examination. Discrimination? Probably. I prefer to think of it as protecting the general public from exhibitions of poor taste. I do not wear skirts myself.

The man with knobby knees was wearing a red pleated kilt, lightweight, a flowing silk blouse, a gray cultured-suede vest and a business cape, more decoration than functional. We don't have weather in Turtledome. And he was built like a lumberjack, half a head taller than me, with shoulders like sides of beef. Therefore, the outfit had to be ceremonial. Or maybe he was just being fashionable. We don't have fashion in the dome either. Jumpsuits mostly, functional and convenient and cheap. Or just lightweight pajamas.

His handshake was surprisingly gentle. "Portal-Master, Carl Lopez, at your service."

I gave him the number three polite-smile-for-intimidating strangers. "Welcome to Turtledome, Portal-Master." I looked around for a chair. We were in the office of Senior Justice Ezra Ben Howell, Grandpa when it wasn't official business. "I'm sorry I'm late, Senior. I had a trial that lasted longer than it should."

"Was it an interesting case, at least? Find a seat, Dar." The Senior wheeled himself out from behind his desk. Right. This was going to be an informal meeting. I parked myself on the couch. The Portal-Master sat down next to me. His knees were not only knobby, they were intimidating.

"Unfortunately not." I explained, "A writer sued her publisher. Poor thing. She didn't know what a can of worms she was opening. All she wanted was her author's copies. But they weren't returning her phone calls. She only filed suit to attract their attention. But, of course, once I had the case, I had to go the distance."

"Of course," scowled Grandpa, crinkling his already well-crinkled forehead. "What did you decide?"

"Well, it was obvious—"

"To me, yes—but maybe not to our guest."

"Sorry, Senior. You're right." To the Portal-Master, I explained, "The whole thing comes under the Corporate Responsibility Code. A corporation can afford to diddle a grievance for years—in fact, it's in the corporation's interest to do exactly that. Precisely the opposite is true for an individual plaintiff. They can't afford to be diddled. Time is the stuff that life is made of. The poor writer didn't even know she was entitled to redress under the code. Fortunately, I did. We gave her two point five in damages, with a double or nothing appeals clause."

"Double or nothing?"

"If the defendant appeals and loses, the award is automatically doubled. Plus penalties," I added. "I suspended the corporation's entire legal department right to Luna for thirty months, they'll have to hire out."

"Isn't that a little strict?" Lopez asked.

"Of course it is. It's supposed to be. They broke the First Rule. They should have handled this a long time ago, but they didn't take it seriously. They kept shrugging it off. After all, it was only a few books. Turned out that the contracts department was responsible for sending out author's copies, and they just didn't want to be bothered." I shrugged. "I really had no choice. People who don't intend to keep their word should not be writing contracts. I also fined the parent company a matching amount, to be paid to the court. A little incentive to keep them honest."

"Sounds like you were annoyed," said Grandpa. He knew damn well I was.

"Of course. This thing should never have come to court. Once it was in my bailiwick, I had no choice but to penalize. The damn corporation broke its word. The only way to make a corporation keep a promise is to make it too expensive to break one. This may keep them honest for a couple of years. Probably won't. Two more complaints of this nature and I'll sign the first petition for public dissolution that comes along. There's absolutely no excuse for deliberate discourtesy."

I added, "Then I fined the writer and her agent half the award for failing to register the contract with an appropriate monitor. She said her Guild was supposed to guarantee enforcement. So I had to double-check that. Sure enough—then I had to fine the Guild too. Failure to perform. I don't know what these people think they're doing. Forming a guild and then not putting teeth in it. Writers! Feh."

I turned sideways on the couch. "Sorry to be so candid, Portal-Master, but having my time wasted makes me cranky."

"Yes, of course." The Portal-Master looked to the Senior Justice. "Yes, you were right. Strict, but fair."

"You picked him out," said Grandpa. "I never said he was pretty."

"Right for what?" I asked. They both ignored my question.

"I'll want a full set of guarantees."

"Naturally," said Ezra.

"Is somebody going to tell me what's going on?" Ezra rolled forward a couple of feet and looked me in the eye. "Portal-Master Lopez is looking to buy a beagle."

I shrugged. "I'm not for sale. You know that, Ezz." To the Portal-Master, I said. "You can rent me—by the hour, week or month, but I'm not interested in a long-term contract, thank you." I did not say that I already had one. That was a family matter.

"Unfortunately, that's the only kind of a contract I can offer you."

"I'm sorry, but I'm really not interested. The only people who can afford to buy an arbiter are corporations. Frankly, I'd rather not be on that kind of leash. Don't get me wrong, I don't hate corporations—but I despise the attitudes they breed in their employees. It encourages them to put their thumbs on the scale. Or worse, they simply dehumanize."

"That attitude is exactly why we want you, or an equally qualified justice, except there aren't any equally qualified. You have degrees in law, economics, and history. And yes, we know you're expensive. That's not a problem. I represent a specific colonial interest. We want—no, we need a constitution, a solid foundation for a future we can't predict, a representative government that can withstand a storm of lies and deceit."

I thought about it. "I'm not sure it's possible. You're dealing with human beings— a species which has deliberately bred itself for arrogance and ignorance. This makes it a difficult uphill battle for anyone who aspires to dispassionate rationality."

"You are not dispassionate," he said.

"Never said I was. But I do aspire to fairness and that has to be enough. At least until we evolve a little bit more."

"Fairness?" Lopez repeated. "Really?"

"The law isn't always fair. Justice has to be."

Lopez considered the thought. "That may be why you're so highly recommended."

"By the Senior? Yes. My grandfather thinks I'm a nuisance. He'll sell me to the highest bidder. So far, I've discouraged most of them." I glanced to Ezz. He kept his expression blank. I turned back to Lopez. "You know, you don't need me. A good intelligence engine can write situation-specific code."

"We know that. Any engine can do boilerplate. But we need something more ambitious."

"I've heard that before too. Mostly from self-appointed revolutionaries. History has more than enough examples of people who've discarded a thousand years of moral evolution—because they're certain they can do it better. That kind of arrogance has brought down three super-powers in this millennium alone. And a few dozen smaller nations too. Also an uncountable number of corporations and businesses that made the mistake of believing in the economic theory du jour."

Lopez looked to Ezz.

"I told you he'd need some convincing," Ezz replied.

Lopez looked back to me. "Right," he said. "That's why we want you. You know what works, what doesn't work."

"Okay, yes. I'm educated. It was easier for my family to send me off to university than to put up with me year-round. I'm not known for my social skills. In case Ezz hasn't told you, I'm somewhere out on the spectrum. But even with the augments, I've never learned how to be nice. No, that's not right. I've never seen the percentage in it. All of which is preface to telling you that I am not interested." I hesitated, thought about it for a moment. "Tell me what you're trying to do. Maybe I'm wrong."

"Thank you," said Lopez. "What you said before. About arrogance and ignorance and failure. How do we build a system that's resistant?"

This time, it was my turn to look to Ezz. He said, "Yep. That's why they picked you. Your high school manifesto."

I shook my head. "I am never going to live that down, am I?"

"Please . . . ?" Lopez said. "We've been struggling with this since before we opened the first portal. How do you establish a representative system of government that cannot be manipulated by wealth or extremism or misinformation or . . . well, anything? How do you protect a democratic republic from its own mistakes?"

I didn't answer immediately. It was a good question. "The obvious answer? You can't. It doesn't matter what safeguards you put in place, the takeover begins when they start saying that this regulation or that one are unnecessary and they whittle it all away. It can take fifty years or longer, but once that first wedge is hammered in, once they open up a crack . . ." I stopped myself. "I don't know. It's an interesting challenge."

"Will you think about it?"

"It's an annoying question. I won't be able to *not* think about it."

"Good," he said. "How soon will you be ready to leave?"

"Huh?"

"The portal train to Praxis leaves Friday

morning."

"Praxis? Wait! What?" I looked to the Senior. "Ezz, help me out here."

"Of course. I'll send someone around to help you pack."

"There's no one else?"

"I'm sure there will be multiple volunteers to help you pack."

"That's not what I meant."

"I know what you meant. I was indulging myself. No, there's no one else. Hart is married. The Fords are both locked into long-term contracts. Harriman . . . no. It's not that You're the only one available, you're the only one specifically qualified." Ezra reached behind himself and grabbed a folder from his desk. "I've taken the liberty of preparing the contracts, Dar." He held it out to me.

"But I—" I stopped. "Ezra, can we talk privately?"

His expression flickered with annoyance, but he nodded toward his private office and rolled away. I followed him in.

"Look, Ezz—" I started to say. "I'm as open-minded as the next man—"

"Like hell you are!" Ezra Ben Howell snapped right back at me. "You're one of the most narrow-minded, tight-assed, martinets I've ever had working in this office. You think I don't remember how you sued your own mother? But you're efficient and you're fair. Which makes you worth any three of the rest. Just spare me the bullshit that you're a sensitive, caring human being and we'll get along fine."

"I love you too, Grandpa—but I can't accept this assignment."

"You don't have much of a choice, Dar. He's got a draft notice. And you're it."

"Oh, shit."

"That's what I said. You think I'm happy about losing you? I've been maneuvering for weeks to keep this fly from landing on my potato salad. Unfortunately—" Ezra looked more annoyed than usual. "—you are the only single, male justice available who has the necessary background."

"But I'm not—!"

"That's what I told the Portal-Master. He said not to worry. You could learn."

"Grandpa!"

"You're thirty-two years old and you're not married, you're not even in a Family right now! What else is he supposed to think? Hell, I've wondered about you myself. In any case, Dar, despite your usual toxic demonstration of your parents' failure to paper-train you, I don't think you've managed to change the Portal-Master's mind. I think he's pretty damned determined to claim your hide."

"It's not my hide I'm worried about."

"Well, unless you can come up with something clever in the next three days, I have no choice but to sign your indenture over to him." He snorted. "I told you not to sue your mother. It was a fool's case to begin with. No way were you going to win."

"This is not fair. I only have twenty-three months left to work off on that indenture. This Praxis thing has got to be a three-year assignment at the very least. I can claim unfair endorsement."

Ezra shook his head. "If you go willingly, Dar, they'll pay off the indenture. If they have to draft you, they'll claim involuntary servitude and reschedule the payoff. You could be there five years."

"How long if I go—you should pardon the expression—'willingly'?"

"Two years, with a six-month option."

"Shit." I paced the room. "Can't you sell me to someone else first?"

"Sorry, they've already registered a claim on you. The Portal-Master is no fool, Dar. He'll slap us both with Draft Evasion if we even try. Do you want to fight Tycho City?"

"Argh! And argh again! This whole damned rock is suffering from an overdose of lawyers!"

Ezra nodded. "Well, look on the bright side. In three days, there'll be one less. At least, you'll be doing a service to those you leave behind."

THE JOB

The situation did have its own bizarre irony.

A starside beagle gets tangled in his own legal suspenders. I'm sure I would have laughed like crazy if it had happened to anyone else.

In the meantime, I had three days in which to tie up my local affairs, one of whom was exceedingly displeased at the situation. As if it were my fault. Well, it was. Kinda. Excellence is its own punishment. So is arrogance.

Had it been any other colony, I would have actually been looking forward to the assignment. Setting up a legal code for a new culture can be a very heady job.

And besides, it would be a break from Luna where there's an overdose of lawyers.

One of the things I learned in Law School was the L-Ratio; Lawyers-to-Lay-People. When it gets above one lawyer per every thousand civilians, you start hitting critical mass. You get irrelevant laws and even more irrelevant lawsuits.

Luna hasn't reached that point yet—unless you count the tourists. In which case, we've not only passed critical mass, we've already imploded. As a matter of fact, more than half of all legal cases on the planet involve tourists or recent immigrants. There's no shortage of ignorance, but it's still not an excuse.

Personally, I've always felt that when a community gets big enough to need a judge, that's the first sign that its outgrown its sense of community. What makes Luna livable is a tradition of keeping the family farms large and the family domes small. The community stays rural and it stays a community.

I can argue the other side of that question too.

It is absolutely impossible to create a stable society without agreements on how the members of that society should behave in regard to one another. Those agreements are called laws. It is a given that the members of a society will always test the applications and interpretations of any agreement—it is a given because people will always test to see how much they can get away with. Call it human nature.

The point isn't that most people hate to follow instructions—most people don't even read the instructions, even when they voted on them in the first place. As a result, any body of law is a continually growing body. The more the laws get tested, the more they grow to cover the contingencies of the test situation. Given a sufficiently litigious culture, the growth of law becomes cancerous.

One of my instructors was quite clear on this, spending several sessions demonstrating how ancient Rome and not-so-ancient America had both succumbed to an overdose of lawyers and Christians. Painful deaths, both.

The law gets unfairly blamed for the inevitable strangulation of society—and not the original breakdown in common courtesy that created the social epidemic in the first place. The failure of courtesy always breeds its own kind of vermin, hyper-litigious hopefuls with hair-trigger lawsuits. This is why judges run out of patience before lunch.

Having practiced law, I have no illusions. Lawyers are the architects of the chaos—especially those lawyers who let such stupid cases get to court in the first place. It's a violation of the First Rule:

The job of the lawyer is to keep the client out of court.

And if the lawyer can't keep the client out of court, then the job is to keep the client out of jail.

Justice is not found in courtrooms—and hiring a judge because you're looking for justice is like hiring a whore when you're looking for love. The best you're going to get is a good performance.

As a Justice-For-Hire, my job is not to dispense justice, but fairness. Which is as close as you can get to justice, this side of Yahweh.

I make recommendations. It's up to the client to implement the recommendations. Some clients don't. In which case, they pay a penalty. It's called a kill fee. Kill fees are very expensive. But then so is my time. I don't like having it wasted. If you hire me, I expect you to use my recommendations, not put them up on the shelf merely because you find them unpleasant or uncomfortable.

I warn my clients ahead of time, "Don't hire me unless you're willing to have your own ox gored. In fact, plan on it." I don't consider a job well done unless everybody twinges a little when they see the result. I can't make everybody happy—that's impossible. What I can do is make everybody equally unhappy. This almost always guarantees a successful implementation. People are happiest when the bad luck is spread around fairly.

I was stupid. It never occurred to me that any of it would end up on my plate.

DINNER

That's what I told Portal-Master Lopez too. Over dinner. His card, my restaurant. The expensive one.

"Listen," I said. "You got the wrong guy. I know nada about monosexual cultures."

He shrugged and examined his salad. "You can learn. I heard you're a quick study."

"I don't have a lot of eagerness for this job, you know."

"Didn't expect you would. Doesn't matter. The job still has to be done."

"Look, you need to understand something." I pushed my half-finished salad to one side.

"Go on," he said.

"I can't do the job you need. I have no background in monosexual law. Never studied any of the enclaves, local or offworld."

The Portal-Master nodded. "Actually, that's an advantage. We need someone lacking empathy, someone who doesn't take sides with anyone, some who is dispassionately alienated—someone like you who insists on making all sides equally unhappy. You are well-respected, even admired, and totally disliked by your colleagues. Even your friends know you don't have any friends. That's an advantage."

"I have never been called an asshole so eloquently."

"We can afford to pay you. Three times your standard fee, plus a 25% cash bonus. And we'll pay off your indenture. We'll give you a Class A household with full service, plus appropriate associates. All we ask in return is a conscientious effort to lay the groundwork for a working constitution, one that avoids the worst traps of the past. Oh, and one other thing."

"There's more?"

"Well, while we have you available, we could also put you on as a senior arbiter. Fully salaried. You'd get to hear a lot of interesting cases and you'd build up your resume. You could return to Luna fully credentialed. You wouldn't have to climb the ladder. You'd leapfrog to the top. You could even run for office. If I understand correctly, you might even outrank your grandfather."

"Really?"

He nodded.

I resumed breathing. "That's a very slick piece of salesmanship, Portal-Master."

"So you accept?"

"Okay, I'm thinking about it. From a personal perspective, it does solve a lot of problems."

"Some of your problems are self-inflicted."

"Yes, Grandpa likes to talk. So does Mom."

"Irrelevant. We vetted you. Thoroughly." He pushed his salad aside too.

"I don't really have a choice, do I?"

Lopez said, "If you are that adamant, I can tear up the draft notice and go back empty handed. We'll look for another candidate. I'm not sure, where, but—"

"Please don't play on my sympathies. I don't have any."

"I know. That's part of why you're right for the job."

The waiter brought our steaks then, and we ate in silence for a bit, broken only by the occasional scrape of knife on plate.

Finally, I said. "Well—?"

He looked up. "Yes?"

"Aren't you going to at least tell me about some of the situations you want resolved?"

"Didn't think you were interested."

"I'm curious about the kind of cases I might be hearing."

"Okay. Try this one. Two co-workers sign a marriage contract. Full partnership, the works. They make two babies. After a few years, the marriage breaks up. Who gets the home? Who takes custody of the children? What are the guidelines for the divorce?"

I shrugged. "Well . . . the contemporary view is that each of the partners in a relationship is entitled to a pro-rata share of the marriage's resources. If there's more than two partners, the size of the shares are determined by the individual's length of time in the family. In your case—I assume it's hypothetical—" I paused to sip at my wine, an Australian Plantagenet Reisling, almost as good as a California vintage. I put my glass down again.

The Portal-Master shook his head. "Not hypothetical. Go on."

"Well in your case—this case—if the Family were on Luna, there wouldn't be a question. I'd say that the house belongs to the children—along with whatever resources were necessary to maintain it. Do you understand the reasoning here? According to the Lunar Code, the primary purpose of a Contract Family must be to provide a safe environment for the raising of whatever children are born to or adopted into the Family until such time as they are of legal age. Whatever other purposes a Family may choose, the rights of the children always take priority. If one parent or the other wants to divorce—fine, no problem. But you don't get to turn the kids into victims."

"Hm," he said.

"This part is personal," I said. "People

should not start babies unless they're planning to train them to be responsible adults. If you don't have the gumption to finish the job you start, you're responsible for the cost of completion. That falls under the heading of responsibility to the community. By extrapolation, the day your first child is born, you've lost your house—and a big bite of your share of the common stock. At least until that kid is eighteen."

"Hm," said the Portal-Master. "Yes. I see the logic." He looked at me. "Does it work?"

"We have a very low divorce rate here. We also have a very low marriage rate. Nobody enlists for the duration unless they mean it. Lots of common-law stuff, though. But wherever there are children the same legal obligations apply."

"Mmm."

"Try another?"

"Sure. Man divorces his partner of twelve years and takes up with a twinkie."

"A what?"

"This year's blond."

"Yeah, okay. I got it."

"—Takes up with a twinkie. A few months later, he dies in an accident. No will. What is the partner of twelve years entitled to? What does the twinkie get?"

"Mm—" I said. "Off the wall, I'd say we'd have to use the same formula as if it had been a three-way marriage, with pro-rata shares to each of the partners. But . . . I'd also want to know the state of the original relationship and which partner wanted to end it. I don't think you could apply a simple formula here, you'd have to adjust it to the individuals. Sorry, I'm pulling a blank."

"Not surprised. That case dragged on for several months. Nobody walked away happy."

"That sounds fair," I said.

Lopez did not look amused.

"Somebody close to you?" I guessed.

"Yeah," he said, and finished his wine. He glowered at me as he put the glass down. "Friday. If you're not there when the train pulls out, I'll tear up your contract. If you are— " He stood up. "Thanks for your conversation, Judge. Now, if you'll excuse me—"

And he was gone.

Somehow, I did not feel better.

STRATEGIZING

S o, I was free. If I wanted to be.

Grandpa might be annoyed for a day or six.

On the other hand, it was an opportunity. I couldn't deny that.

The money was good, the advancement was considerable, the cases would be challenging, and I might come away with a solid credential.

So why was I resisting?

One thing about Luna, the gravity is one-sixth of Earth. This is both good and bad. The good part is that I could hang upside down to think without feeling that my head was going to burst. The bad part is that I had to spend at least two hours a day in the centrifuge to keep my muscles and bones from deteriorating.

Praxis had a near-Earth gravity, I wouldn't need the centrifuge. But Praxis had no women. But then again, I hadn't attempted a serious relationship since law school.

(Sidebar: Do not ever again attempt a relationship with a law student, male or female. Of course, many of them said the same thing about me, so that was fair.)

There's a thing I learned in law school about how to strategize a case. Make two lists. One list is all the things that the other side can use against you. The other list is all the things that you can use against the other side. Now compare the two lists. That will tell you who's likely to win.

If the case goes through an intelligence engine, as most of them do, you'll get a foundation for a settlement. But intelligence engines don't consider the emotional factor in a case. The poor widow with three children might not have grounds, but the greedy landlord is going to lose anyway—especially if it's a jury trial. So you have to put that on both lists.

This trick has nothing to do with law. It has everything to do with winning.

I did that now. I made a list of all the advantages and compared it with the list of disadvantages.

I studied the two lists for a long time.

ORIENTATION

Lopez sent me a very thick package to review and I spent most of the day spelunking my way through it. Transmitting information by personally delivered hardcopy is one of the best ways to ensure that unauthorized persons will not be able to access the information.

Some of it was public knowledge.

Some of it was not.

Praxis is listed as a shirtsleeve world, but not completely. Time-dilation effects are minimal. It is possible to visit Praxis and return home afterward. But only if you don't go outside.

Temporary residents on Praxis, like I intended to be, get quartered in separate chambers, all connected, but all sealed against the outer environments.

As long as you stayed Earth-sealed (the polite term for quarantine) or only ventured out in a suit, you could return to the Seven Worlds.

Once you've stepped outside and been exposed to the native air, you become a permanent resident. You're outed. You can't go back in. You're broken the seal and you're here for keeps. This is the strictest rule of shirtsleeve worlds—it's to prevent the introduction of any invasive species, especially micro-organisms that could be dangerous or disruptive to the already unbalanced ecologies of other worlds. Especially Earth. Three viral outbreaks later.

I would wear a monitor, to validate that I had stayed inside the sealed environments. As I had no intention of going outside, that would not be a problem. One of the reasons I left Indiana was the unpredictability of winter snows and summer tornadoes. Praxis had weirder weather, its orbit was still a matter of argument because it disobeyed the known laws of physics. There were astronomers and mathematicians here just to study the anomaly.

Lopez had included a history of the more troublesome cases that had popped up in the Praxis legal system—troublesome because nobody was happy with the outcome. Some of the cases were still pending and the local administration believed I could help resolve them. Apparently, Praxis did not yet have a Supreme Court. The locals were struggling.

All I had to do was stay inside and work, which was my intention anyway. Did I repeat myself? Yes. Eventually, I would return home.

free of my indenture and quite a bit richer. All I had to do was hear some cases and help design a fascist-proof constitution.

The Constitution of Praxis—that promised to be a much bigger problem. Lopez wasn't a historian, but he was literate, and he wasn't the only one. The elected coordinators of Praxis had been arguing with the Portal Authority coordinators about the kind of legal system they needed since two days after the first punch was thrown, which was two days after the Portal was opened. It was one of those stupid self-righteous arguments fueled by beer and stupidity.

(Tractor Driver X tried to tell Mechanic Y that he was cute. Mechanic Y did not want to be touched—well hugged. Engineer Z, the partner of Mechanic Y stepped in to intervene. And then the friends of X, Y, and Z got involved. All of them had their contracts cancelled and were sent back on the first Portal train.)

The consequences must have seemed severe to the participants, and probably a lot of onlookers as well, but the more important precedent was set. If you left your integrity at home, you would be sent back to find it. Second chances were possible . . . maybe.

Lopez had provided a lengthy document about the goals of the colony and what the new constitution would have to address. I scribbled some notes, but nothing definite. There was a lot of useful boilerplate I could draw upon, but the hard part would be creating a structure that could withstand the assaults of time and stupidity.

THE CHALLENGE

Stupidity is inevitable.

That's why history repeats itself.

Because most people don't learn from history.

Throughout history, what are the most human problems?

This was not an easy question.

I scribbled some thoughts.

Greed.
Selfishness.
Loneliness.
You can't get enough of what you don't really want.
Cruelty.
The need to control the environment.
Reaction to unpleasant circumstances.
Addictions.
Violence.
Damaged people damage people.

No. These were symptoms. Not the disease.

None of them explained anything.

Lack of empathy.

Well, yes. Maybe. But how do you write empathy into a constitution? If you have to depend on the inherent empathy of the species, you're doomed before you start.

The Roman Colosseum proved that. The slavery of captured peoples. Multiple instances of genocide. The industrial murders of the Holocaust. Humanity's endless wars depended solely on the othering of whole populations, the way classes of people were regarded as lesser. It was all the cowardly reaction to anything different.

I leaned back in my chair, my familiar comfortable chair that I would be leaving behind tomorrow morning—I leaned back and studied the ceiling.

"I don't think there's a solution," I said.

And then I stopped myself.

"Dammit."

Because I knew I'd been handed a challenge I couldn't resist.

THE TRAIN

I showed up. I had my laptop, a spare tablet, several libraries on chips, and clean underwear. My suitcase followed politely after me.

Lopez looked up from the tablet he was studying. "Good morning, Dar."

"I thought you'd be surprised."

He shrugged. "If I wanted to gamble, I'd go to Tycho."

"The casinos are rigged."

"Yes. That's why I didn't go to Tycho." He pointed. "You're in Red Three. I'll come see you after we're underway."

The pods were color-coded. The one-way pods, the ones that would be opened on the surface, were green. The conditional pods were yellow. The pods for Praxis' sealed environments were painted bright red.

I walked down the platform, trying not to think about what I was leaving behind, what I would soon be missing. Several good restaurants, a few people who didn't find other things to do when they saw me approaching.

Red Three had a check-in desk, but before I could even flash my passport, the two young men at the counter stood up respectfully. "Welcome, Arbiter." A dark-skinned fellow stepped out of the pod to greet me. "You have a suite and an office. I'll show you the way." He frowned past me. "Is that all your luggage?"

"I wasn't planning on going to the ball."

He didn't smile, maybe he didn't get the joke. "I have been assigned as your associate. Follow me please."

Every pod in a train is a self-sufficient vehicle. Each one is a large pill-shaped car, with three or four levels of accommodations, equipment, supplies, and cargo, with large screens everywhere instead of windows. The pod was triple-hulled and internally reinforced. The structural integrity had to be severe because a portal-train could go through many different environments, low-grav to high, null atmospheric pressure to high, null-radiation to high, null-this and null-that to high this and that.

But inside, a pod would have ample comforts. Passengers might have to spend weeks or even months in transit, depending on how far up the line they were going and how much traffic through each portal. The longest part of the trip would be waiting for clearance to proceed.

My associate who didn't smile led me to a suite with its own kitchen and a connecting office. "This is reserved for people of importance," he said.

Something in his voice. I turned to look at him. "You don't approve?"

"It's not my place to have an opinion." He pointed around. "You should be comfortable here. If you have any questions or special needs, you can call me at any time—"

"Wait," I said.

He paused. "Yes?"

"Sit down?" I pointed to the table and chairs. They looked comfortable.

He hesitated, then sat. I sat down opposite him. Yes, the chair was comfortable.

"Do you want something to drink?"

He shook his head. "Do you? I can get you —"

I waved him back down. "Listen," I said. "Whatever you might have heard about me, or whatever instructions you have, just put them aside for a moment. I don't need a slave. I don't need a servant. I just need an occasional bit of . . . well, let's call it advice. Or consultation. Information. Whatever. And an occasional sense that I'm not some invading alien thing. So whatever else is going on, I need honesty. Otherwise . . ." I spread my hands, "the job will be harder for everyone."

He didn't answer.

I sat back in my chair and looked at him. He was young enough to be at university. He was dark and a little stocky. He did not look as if he had any augments, but he might have been chipped. He had clear skin, dark eyes, close-cropped curly hair, and a face without expression. He waited expectantly.

"What's your name?" I asked.

"Kai."

"Thank you. And you may call me Dar."

"Thank you, Arbiter, but I have been told to call you by your title."

"Is there some reason that you resent me? Or this job?"

He shook his head.

"I asked for honesty."

He didn't answer.

"Look, if you're not happy here—"

"Are you asking for a replacement? If I'm not a suitable associate—"

"Let's start at the beginning. Why were you assigned to be my associate?"

He took a breath. "They felt I would be the best qualified."

"Why? No, wait. Who decided?"

"Portal-Master Lopez. He's also head of the Constitution Committee. It wasn't a job he wanted. But everybody on Praxis takes on two or three responsibilities because there are more jobs than people, so they stuck him with this one."

"Ahh, I see. And he chose you to be my associate because . . . ?"

"Um. He thought that you and I would be a good match."

"Why?"

Kai hesitated.

"Go on."

"He said I'm smart enough."

"What else . . . ?"

Kai cleared his throat, embarrassed. "He said my social skills were almost as bad as yours."

I blinked. I replayed the words in my head. Then . . . I started laughing.

Now it was his turn to blink in confusion. "Why is that funny?"

"It is. It just is."

"I don't understand."

"Think of it this way. I'm your punishment. You're mine." That confused him even more.

I stood up. He stood up with me. I stepped forward and put my hands on his shoulders. I don't normally touch people, but this time was different. I needed to connect. "Look at me. I am who I am. You are who you are. We both have jobs to do. Let's just do them—and surprise everyone. Okay?"

He nodded. "Will there be anything else, Arbiter?"

I let go of him. "No, I guess not."

"I will be back before departure. There

might be a delay, but we should be rolling by eighteen-thirty. That's what they're saying. Is there anything you'd like for dinner? There's a menu on the desk."

"Thank you, I'll be fine."

He left. I shook my head. I did not like slavery, even the legal fiction of indenture. This boy bothered me. Either he'd been hurt or indoctrinated or both.

A
CONVERSATION

The bed was comfortable enough for a short nap.

One of the things about living on a Lunar clock, you don't do night and day like dirtsiders.

You take short naps. You get up and work, you eat, you shit and shower, you work an hour or two, you take another short nap. You alternate work with naps and you develop your own specific relationship with time.

Sometimes you have responsibilities. Be here or be there at a certain hour—that's why you have a clock to remind you. "It is time to prepare for a hearing. Would you like to hear the facts of the case?"

"No, thank you. What's for lunch?"

"Shrimp salad, iced tea. Chocolate crepes

for after. White wine. Coffee."

I didn't expect the pod kitchen to be as well equipped as Turtledome, but the menu was a pleasant surprise. Apparently, the long-distance pod trains usually had a farm-pod to produce fresh vegetables, eggs, and fish. It was also a convenient way to deliver food crops to stations on the track.

We still hadn't left by eighteen-thirty, another delay. Lopez arrived to explain. "We contracted for three more cargo pods. One for Praxis, two to be delivered. They're on their way. We should be out of here by midnight."

"Thanks for the update."

"How are you getting along with Kai?"

"He showed me how to log into the system and hung up my spare shirt. I could have done that myself. I don't think he likes me."

Lopez said, "He doesn't have to. It's not his job."

"What is his job?"

"Bodyguard."

"Huh?"

"I don't want you getting killed."

I didn't know what to say in response to that, so I just stared at him.

"Praxis is an unfamiliar world and human beings are inventive. There are a lot more ways to die on Praxis than there are on Luna. We have a saying, 'Everyone is entitled to one fatal mistake.' Kai's job is to keep you from making yours."

"Oh."

"Do you want him replaced? With someone more likable? I can arrange it. I'm not sure you would be safer though."

I shook my head. "Since you put it that way, no. I don't need him to be charming. Just efficient."

Lopez nodded. "Oh, he'll be efficient. Annoyingly so. That's why I chose him for you."

"Thank you."

"So you're good here. You're ready for Praxis." He looked at me sharply. "You could still change your mind . . ."

"Why should I?" I pointed around the suite. "I'm not paying for this. You are."

"Not me. The Coordinating Committee."

"Tell them I appreciate it."

He shrugged. "There's a lot at stake. So . . . when do you think you'll start to work?"

"I already have."

"Eh?"

I pointed to the table and chairs. We sat down opposite each other. "See, here's the thing. You got me thinking."

"Isn't that what we hired you to do?"

I waved it away. "It's not about a monosexual culture. It couldn't be. After two days of serious research, I couldn't find a workable precedent. There aren't any. Prisons? No. Military institutions? Not really. Homosexual communities? Maybe, but no. Why?

Because all of those environments are as much about the absence of women as they are about men. A true monosexual culture would be a totally different context. And I'm not sure it's one that anyone can create, because humanity is essentially a heterosexual species, no matter how many different ways we try to rechannel it. So that's a tunnel down which there is no cheese."

"He frowned. "If that's the case, then why are you here?"

"Because the question you asked is not the question you need answered."

"Go on." He waited for me to continue.

"Right. You said you wanted a government that couldn't be subverted by time and stupidity. I'm not sure that's possible. But I couldn't stop thinking about it. I still can't. The problem is that every mechanism that you could put in place to protect the workings of any agency or institution or authority—any mechanism can be subverted. As Saint Harlan said, more than once, 'The two most common elements in the universe are hydrogen and stupidity.'"

"So, you're saying there's no solution."

"There is, but it's only a solution if the people want it to be a solution. So that's where my thinking went next. How do you create a sustainable context of institutional responsibility? You can only do that if you create a sustainable context."

"Uh—" Lopez frowned at me again. "That sounds a lot like circular reasoning."

"Oh, it definitely is." I leaned back in my chair. "Can I get you something to drink?" I waved for the service bot. "I'll have lime-seltzer. Cold." I looked to Lopez. "And you?"

"The same. Go on."

We waited while the bot poured the drinks.

When it rolled away, I continued. "It's about the culture you create. It's about the relationship that the people have with their community. They have to feel a connection. 'This is me. This is mine. It takes care of me, I take care of it.' That's the strength of any institution. Destroy that and you destroy the institution."

"That seems obvious."

"So far, yes. But communities change with time. They evolve. Internal pressures. External. Or both at once. That puts pressure on the community to evolve. If it's flexible, it will. If not, then anything that fractures the fundamental relationship is a lever for extremists. The community has to assimilate it or destroy it—or be destroyed in turn. That's the threat that any subversive movement represents. If it can break the relationship, it can topple the whole thing. We have a lot of historical examples. Some of them are in play right now.

"So this is the question you want answered. Part of the question. Can any institution recover itself after the subversive movement gains traction? Maybe. Sometimes. Sometimes not. It depends on the underlying foundations. But after an assault on the structure, you can't go back to the same structure. You have to rebuild it in response to the assault."

Lopez held up a hand to stop me. "Wait. You're going too fast. I hear you. Give me a minute to understand. You're saying if I get punched, I can get back up, but I have to be aware of how you punched me. And watch out for the next one."

"Interesting analogy, but yes."

"So recovery is possible?"

"Recovery requires a revolution. Not necessarily violent. Peaceful revolution works better. A shift in context. A different awareness. An expanded consciousness. A transformation. Call it what you will, you can't go back. You have to adapt. Anyway, if I'm hearing you correctly, what you want is a structure than can include dissent and disagreement, and adapt to circumstances without destroying itself. Am I correct, so far?"

Lopez hesitated. "It's a good start."

"But—?"

"Well . . . Praxis is a population in flux. Maybe population is the wrong word. We don't think like a community. We don't have stability. Some of us want it. Others, not so."

"Explain?"

"The people I represent, we want a social structure. Other people, they talk about different possibilities. They see the opportunities for growth. There are corporations that have invested in the colony and they view Praxis as an opportunity for expansion."

"You're talking about wannabe oligarchs, right? Back on Luna, we called them greedy bastards. Didn't stop them though. Didn't even slow them down."

"Luna is too close to Earth. You couldn't stop them. We're a lot farther out, but it's the same problem. The companies have sunk a lot of money into Praxis, it's a very promising world. It wouldn't be a problem if all they wanted was a fair return. They don't. They want to own the whole planet."

"A fair return? Yes, that's doable. No problem. Define that return and put in strict limits. But if you don't enforce your limits, it doesn't matter what kind of government you create. It'll be irrelevant by the third stockholder's meeting." I looked across at him. "And that's why you need me now—before they install their own authority, right?"

"Your grandfather was right. You're smart enough to be dangerous."

"It's a virtue, yes. But I can live with it."

"Yes, you're charming," he said. "Can you solve the problem?"

"If I have an accurate understanding, and if it's solvable, and if—"

"Yes. And if pigs could fly, we'd need umbrellas." Lopez leaned forward intensely. "We're running out of time, Arbiter. We need to have our legal authority established in the next election. Eighteen months away. We need the mechanism for an election and we need candidates who are aligned with the constitution that you've been hired to write. And we need a mechanism for ratification."

"Oh. You make it sound hard."

"Huh?" Lopez looked surprised.

"It's not hard. It's impossible." Abruptly, I realized something. "You've got an immigration scheduled. You want your legal authority in place before the next wave arrives with their own opinions how the colony should be run, right?"

"Close enough. Yes. The people I represent, the people who sent me, are concerned with a known phenomenon, that too often the creators of a possibility end up at odds with those who arrive into that created possibility and too often reinvent it in their own image."

"Don't be polite, Portal-Master. Say it in dog-shit English."

He nodded. "The corporations are starting to bring in their own people. Their goals are specific."

"I see."

Lopez went on, "At the moment, the population of Praxis is small enough and we have a majority of alignment. But we also know that Praxis needs to grow. We need a population of at least a hundred thousand to achieve self-sufficiency, and we have to create a culture, our own culture, strong enough to resist the intentions of the companies. We can't afford to fraction like—" He pointed upward, vaguely toward Earth.

"Yes, like that," I agreed. "But remember, the species started out fractured, ten minutes after climbing out of Olduvai Gorge."

"You said you've already started working —"

"I'm studying the problem."

Lopez sat back in his chair and looked at me. "Go on."

"All right. Here. Consider this. A democracy is based on the very noble idea that any nation that declares itself to be of the people, by the people, and for the people also has to be accountable to the people. That sounds good, doesn't it? If you have a well-informed and well-educated population, it should work. But too often, it doesn't."

"Because . . . ?"

"A sustainable democracy is an impossible challenge. Mostly because it becomes a target. it requires one thing more than a well-informed population, it requires a sustainable standard of living. Lose that and the democracy implodes. Quickly. Now, a colony is different. It needs an institutional tit to suck on, a nation, a corporation, an ideology—and it only survives if achieving self-sufficiency is built into the plan. As soon as it's self-sustaining, whatever government it establishes, that's when subversion becomes possible, even inevitable."

Lopez thought about it. He pushed his drink around the table for a moment, as if repositioning it might help him organize his thoughts. It left a wet trail of condensation. Finally, he looked across at me. "Okay, so how do you protect it from subversion—from extremists?"

"That's the point, you can't protect anything from extremists—because extremists are fanatics and fanatics always have aggressive, far-reaching plans. Most of them fail, but sometimes you get a fanatic with enough intelligence to recognize that any takeover requires first that you take over all the safeguards and safety nets." I pointed up, vaguely toward the Earth. "There is no shortage of examples. The obvious ones, yes, but there are too many that are not so obvious."

"Please tell me you have an answer for that?" He looked across at me. "Do you?"

"Maybe. But first you have to understand the problem—there's one specific tool that extremists always use. Bullshit."

"Eh?"

"Sorry, that's a technical term. It means lies. Propaganda. Misinformation. Gaslighting. Bullshit works even better in places where there is fear, anger, and desperation. And if those three things aren't available, then you have to create them. But regardless, extremists need carefully targeted bullshit to create the appearance of an ideological imperative and from there, they can create a political movement. Or if it's convenient, and it usually is, they can take over a religious movement and channel that into a political force. But the goal is always movement. Not just movement—momentum. Real momentum. And then—"

"Go on," he said, leaning forward.

"—once a movement has momentum, it becomes a blob. It assimilates, takes over, replaces, or simply destroys anything in its path that might function as an obstacle—schools, media, courts, legislative bodies, even charismatic voices—because ultimately the goal is to capture the existing power structure, suspending or ending all previous agencies and authorities. So the question isn't, how do you safeguard against extremism? It's how do you safeguard against bullshit? Propaganda, lies, misinformation. Bullshit."

"And . . . ?"

"You can't."

"Eh?"

"Not if you want to guarantee the right of free speech."

Lopez hesitated. His expression clouded. "Why do you have to be so goddamned smart?" he said.

"Sorry about that. No, I'm not sorry at all."

His expression went serious. "Is there an answer?"

"I'll give you one you won't like, nobody does." I said, "Free speech is not a right. It's a responsibility. In fact, maybe that's how you'll want to write your new constitution. Instead of a Bill of rights, a Bill of Responsibilities. What do you think?"

"Hard to enforce."

"Make it a condition of voting. Establish a constitutional literacy test. You have to pass it to vote. And make the requirements even more rigorous for those who want to hold office."

Lopez looked at the time. He pushed himself to his feet, shaking his head. "That is not going to go over well."

"Probably not. But I think that's where you should start."

DEPARTURE

The pod-train didn't start rolling until oh-three-hundred. I was napping again, having a surreal dream about the tunnels under Turtledome and all the little stalls and shops that lined the walls, selling diaphanous wings and bright-painted flyboards, frothy gelatins and puffed-rice sushi, colorized moon-suits and sparkling reflection capes, all of that —but the movement of the train brought me awake.

I sat up and looked at the large screen opposite. We were rolling across the Lunar plain toward the first Portal.

Some people find the stark white surface of Luna beautiful. Others find it disturbing. Most of it is tedious. It isn't until you get to the mountains or the rills that that the scenery becomes impressive, even frightening. It's easy to imagine that there might be dangerous things lurking out there, hiding in the black shadows.

But Luna is lifeless and mostly sterile. There are some things that can survive the unforgiving vacuum, like tardigrades, but no boojums yet.

The bigger hazard here is the low gravity. If a person doesn't portal back to Earth regularly or spend time in the public centrifuges, they lose muscle mass and bone density. Other organs get lazy too. In low-grav, the eyeball gets rounder so eyes change their focus. Without the stronger pull of gravity, the sense of balance shifts. Muscles accustomed to one gee overreact. That's why ceilings are padded on Luna.

Even people over a hundred Earth years who've come here for enhanced mobility still have to exercise. For them, immigration is a one-way trip. They're not going back. Loonies like to tell them, "You'd be better off on Mars." It's a friendlier adjustment, but it's the same problem of environmental sustainability wherever a body ends up. Survival requires air, water, food, shelter, and an occasional reassuring hug.

Hmm. That might be another thing to consider for Praxis. The cost of personal maintenance. What does a person owe the community that makes survival possible? I crossed to the desk and dictated a quick note.

Kai came in while I was still dictating. He glanced briefly at my nakedness, then went to the closet and brought me a robe. I nodded a thank you and continued dictating. He waited patiently.

I said, "Pause," and turned to him. "Yes?"

"We're fifteen minutes away from the first portal. I have to secure everything."

I looked around. "There's nothing to secure."

"I'm required to check, if you don't mind."

I shrugged. "Do what you gotta do."

He didn't move. "One more thing. Will you be wanting breakfast?"

"Is that part of your duties?"

"My job is to ensure your well-being."

"But you don't have to like it."

"We've already established that, haven't we?"

"Yes, we have. And I appreciate your honesty. Maybe one day, you will appreciate mine. And yes, I will have breakfast."

"I'll serve you after the transfer. Can you handle the shift to Martian gravity? Or would you like some assistance?"

"I spent two weeks on Earth a month ago and I've ridden the one-gee centrifuge for at least ninety minutes or more, three days a week. I've been to Mars twice. I should be okay."

"Just the same . . ."

"Okay, fine. Yes, you can sit with me."

He bounced out.

Low-grav affects the way a person walks. Human beings walk by leaning ahead, then putting a foot in front of themselves to keep from falling. Repeat until you get where you're going. The lower the gravity, the farther forward a person has to lean to shift their balance forward. Toddlers don't do that, they stagger. They actually have to learn to run before they can learn to walk. At least on Luna, you fall down a lot slower.

But that's why videos of people on Luna look funny to people on Earth. Everyone is leaning forward and it looks like they're running. And bouncing. Martian gravity is one-third, so the difference isn't as extreme. Still, the shift is noticeable. People who travel back and forth a lot are better able to adjust. Others need a little more time to get used to the change. And if you go from lighter to heavier, you can expect some muscle soreness for a few days.

The screen announced our approach to the portal. The train had entered a tunnel and was descending deep beneath the surface. Most stations are triple-airlocked on both sides of the portal. Most are also in a hardened containment. And most are buried deep enough that if there is a blowout, the containment can be safely imploded. Lessons learned hard after the Montana disaster.

Every portal is an opening between vastly different environments. Gravity is the most noticeable, but atmosphere, air-pressure, and radiation levels are also factors. That's why every pod has to be self-sufficient.

Kai came back and sat down opposite me. Neither of us had much to say. It was clear that he had spent a lot of time traveling between multiple gravities. As soon as we transferred to Mars, he was up again and moving around like a native.

When I mentioned it, he said, "I grew up on a wheel. My parents worked the whirligig, throwing cargo around the belt."

"And you wanted more?"

"The portals made slingshots redundant. Unprofitable."

"If there's a portal in place, yes. The expense can be significant."

"The initial expense, yes. But the convenience of immediacy makes it worth it. There's still a need for whirligigs, hurling portals to new locations, and a lot of cargo too, but it's a niche market now. It's all about economics, isn't it?"

I nodded in agreement. "That's the problem I'm dealing with. How do you create a government that can't be bought?"

Kai frowned. "That's not possible. Is it?"

"I don't think it is. But maybe it's possible to make it too expensive to buy."

MARS

We had a three-day layover on the red planet, picking up more cargo, delivering some, and waiting for our place in the transportation schedule. We'd lost our previous slot because of the delays on Luna, which had been caused by delays on Earth, which had been caused by the fact that everything is connected to everything else.

The fellow who sneezes on Tuesday causes the butterfly to flap its wings in China on Thursday which is why the tornado in Texas derailed the train on Sunday. That's why your coffee cost three cents more on Wednesday.

Something like that.

The result was that we had a couple of extra days prowling the corridors of Bradbury. Kai was my guide, or maybe I was his. We did not get to Wells or Welles-With-An-E or Burroughs, but we did take the cable car up to the top of Olympus Mons for an overnight at *Chateau*

Martien. It's a long ride, but the view is amazing. Kai had never done it and this would be my last chance for a while. I still thought the restaurant was overpriced, but the food was good, mostly homegrown.

In the souvenir shop, we both laughed at the toy Martians, little green men with enlarged skulls, big black eyes, and silvery tunics. I bought him one.

"What's this?" he asked.

"It's a souvenir."

"But why are you giving it to me?"

"Because you laughed."

"It's silly." He frowned, not really understanding.

"You've never had a gift before?"

He didn't answer.

"Look at the date. December 25th. Merry Christmas."

He shook his head and handed the little green Martian back to me. "I don't believe in that."

"Okay," I said. "But keep it anyway."

"Why?"

"Because I asked you to. Because it's important to me."

He shrugged and put it in his bag. We moved on.

The museum had a display of old-fashioned predictions about life on Mars and Luna, mostly huge transparent domes protecting marvelous cities and parks. It must have seemed logical, certainly impressive, but it ignored the reality of living without a protective atmosphere.

Most of the settlements on the red planet are dug in deep to protect against micro-meteor impacts. Anything larger, gets tracked and vaporized before it becomes a threat, but micro-meteors are sometimes too small to detect.

There are some domes, of course, mostly because the tourists expect them, but real Martians dig in. As on Luna, there are cable cars out to the smaller settlements, and some of those are worth the trip.

Kai wasn't much for conversation. Neither was I. If I wasn't explaining a point of law, there wasn't much else I could talk about. So mostly we just sat and looked at the scenery. Mars is somewhat more interesting than Luna. It has sunsets, of a sort.

One thing did happen though, and I wasn't sure what it meant, but on the way back down from *Chateau Martien,* we shared the cable car with a gaggle of Earth tourists. One of the women leaned forward to ask, "Are you two a couple?"

Before I could shake my head, she said, "Whatever you're fighting about, it's not important. Talk to each other."

I nodded and thanked her

noncommittally. I wasn't going to explain. But a few moments later, Kai reached over and held my hand. He held it all the way down to the terminal and all the way back to the pod. But as soon as we were inside, he let go and disappeared off to his own quarters. I didn't see him again until dinner time.

"May I ask—"

He didn't answer. He continued setting the table. Finally, he uncovered the casserole dish in front of me. Martian stew. Of course. Rice, beans, noodles, mushrooms, sausage, peppers, tomato sauce, shredded cheese, with sour cream and oyster crackers on the side.

"There's more than enough here. Join me?"

He shook his head.

"Please?"

He hesitated, nodded, and put another plate on the table. He filled both plates, then seated himself opposite.

"Did you have a good time today?"

He nodded.

"It's all right to talk to me."

"I know. I just don't have much to say."

"You held my hand."

"I apologize."

"There's nothing to apologize for. I liked it."

"That's not why I did it."

"Did you like it?"

"That's not important either."

"Then why?"

"Appearances. That's all."

"Oh."

We ate in silence for a bit.

"Y'know," I began, "I've never cared much about appearances. I've never had to."

He put his fork down. "I don't want anyone to think I'm your servant or your assistant or any kind of follower. If they think I'm your partner, my job will be easier."

"And mine?"

He shrugged.

I put my fork down. "I'm a lawyer. Part of my job is knowing when someone is telling the truth. Or not. You're prevaricating."

"What's prevaricating?"

"In your case, withholding evidence. What's going on?"

He didn't answer. He was thinking it over. He looked across at me. "I was supposed to go shirtsleeve. They said yes, then they said no, then they gave me to the Portal-Master and he brought me here to be your . . . whatever."

"Shirtsleeve?"

"There are three populations on Praxis. The shirtsleeve people are the permanent ones. They're never going back to Earth or anywhere they might carry an invasive microbial population. They're the ones who actually go out into the world, exploring, surveying, building, doing things.

"Then there are the temporary people, the semi-permanents, the ones living in sealed environments, never exposed to the outer world. Like Portal-Master Lopez. It's part of his job, but it doesn't matter how loyal to Praxis any of the temporary people might be or how long they've been on Praxis—any time they want to, they can go back. And a lot of them do. The Portal-Master spends a lot of time traveling. Maybe too much."

"Uh-huh. And the third population?"

"Tourists, inspectors, shareholders, corporate sponsors, all the people who come to visit. They never step outside, not even in suits, they just poke around for a bit, eat our food, breathe our air, flush our toilets, and then go back to Earth or wherever and make their reports thinking they know something about us."

"I see. And you regard me as a member of that third group."

"Yes."

"Even though I've been drafted to write a constitution?"

He shrugged. "It doesn't matter what you write. The people of Praxis are going to decide what we want. Not you."

I wasn't sure how to respond to that. I covered by taking a sip of wine. It wasn't bad wine. Martian grown grapes. I looked across at Kai. His resentment was clear.

"Thank you," I said. "Thank you for your honesty." I put my wineglass down and added,

"You might be right. Whatever I come up with, it still has to be voted on. If I understand correctly, Portal-Master Lopez is only one part of the Coordinating Committee. So . . . there's that."

He shook his head as if everything we'd said was irrelevant. He picked up his fork and resumed eating.

"Look," I said. "Neither one of us wants to be here. We both had other plans. But here we are, so let's just . . . I don't know, let's just do what's in front of us and get it over with and then we can both get back to our lives."

"Yeah, okay."

"Just one other thing."

"What?"

"Next time you hold my hand, do it because you want to, not because you have to."

Maybe he nodded. I wasn't sure.

We finished the meal in silence.

OUTBOUND

From Mars, we went to the asteroid belt. Ceres had only 3% Earth gee, so everything had to be strapped down. From Ceres, we leapt to Sedna in the Oort Cloud. That was even smaller, only 1% gee.

But now we had a clear track outward and rolled through the next three outbound portals in a single day. We didn't have any cargo to deliver and nothing to pick up, so we just kept going.

Mirabel was a mining world, a barren lifeless rock, far enough out from its primary that it was covered with nitrogen ice, but beneath the ice, there were useful metals, gold, nickel, iron, platinum, and more. It was valued at nine quintillion plastic dollars. Because it had no life, because it was unsuitable for terraforming, nobody worried about pollution. The machines dug, Other machines processed. Ingots of ore went upline and down. The money flowed back to the companies that ran the machines.

Socrates was a gas world. Frozen carbon dioxide, frozen oxygen, frozen argon, frozen nitrogen, frozen neon, and frozen helium, even frozen hydrogen, all organized in nice convenient layers. The gas market was almost as profitable as the mineral market, but it required specialized containers for each of the gases.

North Station was a transfer station, a low-grav asteroid, smaller than Sedna, but it hosted a serious vacuum factory. They made lift balls—nearly indestructible polygraphene spheres and cylinders with literally nothing inside, floating toys at first but the engineering possibilities were enormous, especially on Earth.

Anywhere you needed to offset weight, you installed lift-balls. They could be manufactured as small as marbles or as large as could be passed through a portal. They could reduce the energy cost of anything that flew, be used for the construction of impossible bridges and buildings, and could even offset the weight of the bottom 60 kilometers of an orbital beanstalk. Architects designed tethered houses that could rise high above the landscape. Engineers built tethered platforms that could rise to the top of Earth's atmosphere for launching satellites or even manned spacecraft. Ships with enough lift-balls embedded into their hulls above the water line were practically unsinkable.

They had little practical use on worlds like Luna where the atmosphere was non-existent, they had some limited use on Mars, but Praxis and other shirtsleeve worlds were already placing big orders. We paused our journey to add three cargo pods to the train.

Elbow-49 was a Titanoid moon circling a gas giant. I don't know how it got its name, I didn't ask. Here they were extracting methane from a mostly nitrogen atmosphere. It had near-Earth gravity. Kai and I both used the transit time for exercise. That's one of the problems with portal trains, the constant changes in gee can confuse a person's internal balance. Regular exercise helps, but that's not always convenient.

Praxis wasn't exactly the end of the line, but it was far enough out one of the branches that the journey could be problematic. Traffic to and from all the other stations was supposed to be carefully scheduled, but any small delay would send ripples of rescheduling throughout the entire system. So even though we were supposed to have a clear track, we didn't always. There were times we had to sit on a sideline and wait for an opportunity to proceed through the next portal.

The time wasn't wasted though. Lopez made frequent visits. I invited Kai to sit in on the conversations. We had sandwiches and tea.

"Talk to me," Lopez said, seating himself, fastening his seatbelt. We were delayed on another airless rock, another convenient transfer station between worlds. None of us wanted to go bouncing around the room.

"Okay, I said. Try this on. What if we stop talking about rights and start talking about responsibilities? So, instead of the right to free expression, what if you have the responsibility of expression instead? You are responsible for what you say and do. You are not free from consequences."

"Isn't that already the case in—?"

"Theoretically, yes. In practice, hah!" I took a breath. "See, the whole conversation about rights has been so badly misinterpreted that too many people confuse rights with license. They think the right of free speech is a license to misinform, propagandize, and outright lie —without consequences. People who say, 'I'm just expressing my opinion,' don't want to be held accountable when they drop turds into the punch bowl. They get offended when you call them on it. No. An opinion, informed or otherwise, is what a person is supposed to stand for, what they're committed to being accountable for. And if not, they it's just noise and they should shut their cock-hole."

Lopez said, "It sounds like you've had some experience with that."

"Tourists from Earth."

"Ah," he said. "Yes, I understand. The inherent disadvantage of living in an environment where you don't have to pay for your air, water is plentiful, and you can walk away from facts. People from Earth rarely recognize their environmental debt." He added, "We don't have that problem on Praxis. We have disagreements, yes, but—"

"Not yet, no. Because nobody gets to Praxis without a lot of pre-education and discipline and rigorous training. You weed out the stupid ones. But once Praxis becomes successfully self-sufficient, you'll breed your own class of idiots. It's inevitable. That's why I'm here. You hope I can suggest some safeguards."

Lopez nodded agreement. "And . . . ?"

"You do not have free expression. You have the responsibility of expression. Speech, entertainment, news, whatever form of communication, you do not have the right or the authority to inflict harm on any other person, place, or thing. The consequence for irresponsible behavior must be appropriate to the offense, including prohibition against further access. I'm not certain yet how to write that into law, the phrasing is tricky, but that's the idea. You want to slow down the liars and propagandists, put a prohibitive cost on the offense. Because if you don't, they'll assume they have license. Fact-checking. Evidence. Research. That's part of the responsibility."

"Is that workable?"

"The mechanisms have to be in place

somehow. Yes, you want to have disagreement. Thesis versus antithesis produces synthesis. That's necessary for any forward movement in ideological evolution, that's what you need to maintain a healthy society. You can't allow the noise to overwhelm the signal. That's how civilizations collapse into barbarism, anarchy, and authoritarian regimes."

"It sounds like you're trying to set up an authoritarian system to prevent an authoritarian system."

"Yes, I figured you'd spot the problem. Nevertheless, you can't have rights without responsibilities in the matter."

"You have suggestions?"

I pointed to Kai. "He gave me an idea. Thank you, Kai."

"Go on."

"Kai said that there are three specific populations on Praxis. Permanents, temps, and tourists. Forget the tourists, they bring money and ignorance. Focus on those who have an investment in permanence. So, your shirtsleeve population, the ones who are permanent residents, their votes have to be guaranteed. The temps? Those who are living in sealed environments and can return to Earth or wherever anytime they want—that's you too. And Kai. You haven't gone outside. You might be committed but you're not fully committed. Whether you think so or not, you still have one foot out the door. But you should have a vote too. Because your goal is to be permanent. So right there, Praxis has a divide. And I'll bet that sometimes it's polarizing. An ideological chasm. Even the roots of a civil war. *Correctamente*?"

Lopez looked uncomfortable. So did Kai.

"I thought so."

They waited for me to continue. "As long as that situation continues, that divide will always be a part of Praxis. Because those two demographics will always have different goals. Your challenge, well my challenge now, is to find a way to create a larger common goal that both sides can commit to. All sides, actually. Even the tourists."

"And . . . ?"

"You're making me do all the work here?"

"That's what we're paying you for."

"Yes, that's true. But you need to be a part of the process. It has to be your solution. Not mine. You won't accept an outsider's opinion. You have to make it yours."

Lopez and Kai exchanged a glance. Finally, Lopez said, "We're stuck. We've been stuck for months. Years. Maybe from the beginning. But we know we're stuck. That's why you're here. To get us unstuck."

I sat back in my chair. I readjusted my seatbelt around my waist. I was going to have to lose a few kilos. I looked across at both of them, perhaps seeing them for the first time. Lopez was stocky and gruff. Kai wasn't gruff.

I looked at them like an arbiter. They had a case. A good case, but a losing case—and they'd come to my court hoping that I could give them justice. Something. Anything.

I felt like a blind man carrying a lantern. Somebody might find their way. Just not me.

I said something I hated saying, "I need to think about this. Let me get back to you."

I hated saying that because too often it meant, "I don't want to think about this at all."

THINKING
ABOUT IT

We rolled through a long dark tunnel, half-gee. I wasn't sure where we were, nothing showed up on the monitors, and when I asked, Kai said, "We're not allowed to know."

"Okay. Can we speculate?"

He shook his head.

"Okay again. What's for lunch?"

We rolled across a sun-blasted desert, half-gee. And from there another ice-world, a gee and half, we mostly stayed seated for that one. Another barren rock, no gee to notice, and after a while I stopped watching the screens that served as windows and focused on the real job, only noticing when the gravity might shift again.

I ate, I slept, I stared at my laptop. I browsed the data files on my tablet. There were no answers there. I flopped back down on the bed.

--and came awake cursing my own stupidity.

Of course.

No wonder I missed it.

Grandpa was right. I am an asshole. Arrogant, selfish, and so wrapped up in myself that I would miss the obvious if it hid in my shoe and stung me to death. Grandpa grew up in New Mexico.

And the answer was simple.

Ask them what they want.

I could make notes about what they needed, but they had to decide what they wanted.

Ahh, that was it.

What they want should not be confused with what they need.

I sat down at my desk.

Needs:
Clean Air
Clean Water
Healthy Food
Comfortable Attractive Clothing
Safe Shelter
Family structure ?
Health Care
Education, (not indoctrination)
Goals, Opportunities, Possibilities

Honest Work (Work that makes a difference.)
Safe Retirement
~~Information~~
Accurate Information
~~Representation~~
Fair Representation
Trustworthy Legal System
Trustworthy Economic Management
Trustworthy Government
Enlightened Cultural Identity
Context
Arts and Entertainment that reflect the context.

Those last few would be a reflection of what a population might want, but wouldn't be possible until all their needs were met.

I studied the list. Had I left anything out? Probably. But these were the obvious.

Air, water, food, everything that could be defined as necessities—these had to be guaranteed, protected, freely available to all.

Well, yes—but there was always someone to self-righteously argue, "Why should I pay for someone else's—" And that one always worked where people were fearful and desperate. But that was the thing that brought down nations, selfishness overriding self-interest.

The answer should have been obvious. Because the alternative is living in a world filled with hungry, desperate, ignorant, people who will happily kill you for your selfishness.

Okay, this was all first semester stuff. Time to do the advanced course.

Government has to regulate clean air, clean water, protecting the food supply, even making affordable housing available. Those are necessary services. Authority and responsibility have to balance. But without economic management—

Ahh, that was it.

The minimum basic income must be equal to the cost of living plus fifteen percent wiggle room. The minimum basic income must be guaranteed to all, and free of taxes. Taxation must only begin above the minimum basic income. The economic health of a society is measured by the lowest class, not the highest. Freedom from economic fear was the best way to prevent a revolution.

Taxes. Yes. A flat tax rate is proportionally unfair to the lower tiers of income. It's proportionally unfair in the opposite direction at the higher tiers. Taxes have to be proportional to income. Why? The more a person is benefitting from their economic participation in the society, the more they owe to its maintenance.

I had to stop there. I could already hear the arguments from the other side.

And to some extent, those arguments were logical—as long as you didn't look at the human cost in ignorance, disease, poverty, and desperation.

Ideally, if an economy is healthy, then every member of that economy should be entitled to share in that health. If a troop of monkeys arrives at a large tree filled with ripe fruit, every monkey in the troop should be entitled to eat, not just the senior monkeys. And if you looked hard enough then human beings were not that far off the evolutionary tree from a troop of monkeys.

It's not about the health of the individual, it's about the health of the population. If the population isn't thriving, it doesn't matter how good the senior monkeys are doing. That population is dying.

I studied my notes for a bit, then rewrote them as a proposal for Article One.

SERVICE

We were an hour out from the last Portal. Lopez came by to let me know what to expect. "The immigrants are in the forward car. They have to be processed. You won't. You and Kai and I, we'll ride this car to a different terminal. There'll be a greeting committee. Smile politely, say nothing."

"I can do that."

"No, I mean it. Say nothing. Not everybody is in your fan club. In fact, nobody is. You're a . . . hmm, how can I say this? You're a black swan."

"Yeah, I kinda figured that." I pointed to Kai who stood by impassively. "He's been candid."

"Yes, that was part of his job too. He asked me just how candid he could be. I told him no holds barred."

"I figured that."

Lopez parked himself at the table and waved to Kai. "As long as you're up?"

Kai took the hint. He brought coffee. Fragrant steam rose from the cups.

I parked myself opposite Lopez. Kai took the third chair and opened a tablet to take notes.

"Okay," I began. "This is first year stuff, but let me cover it anyway. The word govern has two definitions. Maybe three if you're picky. The first definition is control. And that's been the historical definition since the invention of the club. The second definition is management, which also means control. The third definition, and this is the one that I think Praxis should use, is service. The purpose of government is to provide services that the people cannot create as individuals."

Lopez nodded as he considered it. "We've had that discussion here. Not in those exact terms though. We've been asking what's the best way to manage a society?"

"That's your mistake," I said. "You're still thinking management. Forget management. Think about service. Anything else is self-righteous bullshit."

"A little colloquial, but I see your point."

"Fail to provide services and you don't have a government, you have a simmering pot of revolution just waiting to boil over." I sipped at my coffee. It was good.

"This is one of the services," I said, indicating my cup. "If I had to live without it, I'd be annoyed, maybe even resentful, but

I wouldn't go to war. Take away eggs, bread, butter, I start to think that maybe something is wrong somewhere. I could put up with a little hardship if you tell me it's only temporary, you're working on it, I can be patient—but the longer the hardship continues, and if it just keeps getting worse, then one day you're overdrawn at the credibility bank. You saw my notes. You saw my rough draft. It's about context. Once that context is destroyed, it can't be recovered. Not by you. Not by any of your colleagues. Context has to be recreated. Reinvented. Context can only be restored by someone who can deliver services. And that'll be a different context than the one it replaces."

"You're talking a different government?"

"A different philosophy of government." I put my cup down. "This is why the list is upside-down. You have to establish context first. Once you establish context, content is inevitable. If your context is control, you get resentment. If your context is service, you get partnership."

"That's a lot to consider."

"True."

"Which means it's a hard sell."

"Even more true."

Lopez put his cup down. "Let me tell you about the men of Praxis. We're stubborn. Especially the shirtsleevers, the neo-natives. They're the ones who've committed to living under the bright blue sun, only retreating from the double winters when the CO_2 lies like frost on the ground, or the broiling summers, the scorch zone across the equator that boils lakes into steam. And the unknown things in the seas, the things that scurry into their burrows on the land, the grass so tall you can get lost in it, the ever-present windstorms, the tornadoes and hurricanes. Calling it shirtsleeve is . . . well, it isn't. But once in a while, it is.

"The rest of us, we're safe inside our tunnels—we're stubborn too, but in a different way. On the surface, it looks like we're short-tempered, cranky, cantankerous, and self-righteous about what we're doing here. We're resistant to outsiders and suspicious of tourists —and that includes you and whatever you might have to say about how we should govern ourselves.

"But you'll also find something surprising here as well. There's a special kind of gentleness here, something that we only share with each other. Call it respect. Call it partnership. Call it commitment or contribution or whatever other jargon you people use. We don't talk about it much because we haven't invented the words for it yet, but we know it's there. Maybe it has to be wordless, because if we turn it into a word, it stops being what it is. Something that belongs to us and no one else."

"Context," I said, and immediately regretted it. "Sorry. But that's how I see it. Praxis is developing a context."

Lopez didn't look annoyed. He considered it. "Yeah. Maybe."

Kai picked up our empty cups. "Fifteen minutes," he said. "Time to lock down."

"Service," said Lopez, nodding. "Yes."

ARRIVAL

The train slid into the last portal, through the triple airlocks, one after the other, then through the portal where we felt the immediate increase in gravity, then we rode through three more airlocks. "Welcome to Portal City," Kai said.

We were still underground, but perhaps not as deep. I couldn't tell. Praxis had a thick atmosphere, more than enough to burn up any micro-meteors, but the extreme variations in weather were a greater challenge. If Praxis had a motto, it was "Dig or split." And the word "split" had multiple meanings here, especially when the razor palms started shedding and the winds picked up the leaves.

Our pod was shunted off to the side. The screens displayed a map and Kai offered his own wry commentary. "The techs work for the corporation. They do their jobs for a few months, then they go home. Sometimes they come back. Not because they like Praxis. They like money. They get paid well for coming this far out. There's no shortage of applicants, but there aren't many who stay long either."

"Why not?"

"No women."

"Really?"

"You should study the demographics. We're not all monosexual. Some of us are here just to get away."

"Some of us?"

He waved the question away. "I was generalizing."

"And get away? From ... ?"

"From all of that." He waved toward the rear of the pod, as if pointing back to Earth. "Everyone has a different story."

"May I ask? What's yours?"

He shook his head. "It isn't important."

"I disagree."

He stared across at me. "Why do you want to know?"

"We have to work together, don't we?"

He didn't answer immediately. He looked off somewhere else. "Praxis isn't the haven that some people think it is."

"I was beginning to figure that out."

"Yes, there is a sense of community here, or maybe a bunch of different communities who've agreed not to kill each other. We don't all share the same . . . I don't know, history.

Not everyone's an immigrant. Some are exiles. You didn't know that, did you? We're supposed to start a new life here. We have to. Because most of us aren't allowed to return. Not just the shirtsleevers."

"Yourself?"

He hesitated. "Yes."

"How did you get here?"

He shook his head.

"That bad?"

"Earth," he said.

"Y'know," I began. "On Luna, and Mars too, we have a low opinion of dirtsiders. Resentment maybe. It's the mother planet, and we're supposed to love it. The poets write about the good green hills of Earth, the longing, the hunger, the freedom to run naked across the fields. All of that. And if all we knew of Earth was the natural beauty of it, yes. But that's not all we know. We see the tall, magnificent cities, yes, but down on the streets, we hear the noise, the chatter, the sirens, the screams, all the traffic noises, the growling of machinery, the roar of engines, the banging and clanging of industry, the smokestacks, the garbage everywhere, the endless sewage, the torrents of waste, and the indifference—as if this was normal. Everybody was so used to all the inefficiencies and inequalities, and ugliness that they accepted it as life. This far out, Earth looks terrifying. And it is. It's not what humans are supposed to be."

"You've been there." It wasn't a question.

"I was born there. Grandpa went to Luna, I followed him and finished law school there. Luna is quieter. I didn't realize how stressful Earth could be until I left it."

"I was born on Earth too."

"Really."

He nodded.

"Somewhere in Ohio, I think. Or maybe Iowa. Or Idaho. My parents moved around a lot. They were—"

"Go on."

"They were Revelationists. You know about Revelationists?"

"Only from a distance."

"Lucky you. They found me in bed with my girlfriend. I was fifteen. She was fourteen. They were horrified. They would have had me exorcised, except that was illegal in that state. So the church declared me incorrigible. And I applied for immigration to get away from all of them. I don't know why Praxis accepted me, but they did and I'm glad. I haven't regretted it. Praxis is better than Earth. Better than my experience of it, anyway."

It wasn't the first horror story I'd heard. And not the worst either. But every horror story is real to the person it happens to. "I'm sorry," I said. "There is a lot of beauty on Earth. I'm sorry you didn't get to see it."

"I saw it. We moved around a lot. There

were a lot of times I thought about running away. I could have. But I didn't have any place to go. Until Praxis."

"May I ask . . . ?"

"What?"

"Praxis is monosexual. Did you rechannel?"

He shook his head.

"Keeping your options open? In case you decide to go back?"

"I'm not going back." Then he added, "I've been with a woman. On Luna too."

"This last trip?"

"Uh-huh," he said. "It was nice. But Praxis has sexbots. They can be individually responsive. If you know what I mean."

"Um. Yes."

For a moment, we just sat and looked at each other, a rare moment of mutual understanding.

Maybe he needed to explain it, to be clear about it—not to me, but to himself. "I might rechannel, someday," he offered. "But only if I met the right guy. If I was attracted. But so far, no."

"Maybe if you rechanneled, you'd be more likely to find someone attractive." I'd heard that a few times. I didn't know if it was true, but I repeated it anyway. It was something to say.

"Yeah, I've heard that." He shrugged. "I think I'll probably have to do it. Eventually. I don't want to end up old and alone."

"I will give you a compliment, Kai. You are smart and capable and while I'm not exactly an expert on these things, I suspect that there are quite a few who will find you attractive. When the time comes. I don't think you're going to end up alone."

He didn't answer immediately. Maybe the conversation made him uncomfortable. Finally, he looked over at me and said, "Thank you."

The pod slid to a halt and the arrival chime sounded. Lopez came up from below, smiling. "Welcome to Praxis."

WELCOME

Kai led me through the tunnels and then the corridors and finally to the suite that had been set aside for me. He said it was new, recently dug into the hillside. I would be the first occupant. I didn't know whether to be flattered or not.

He pointed. "Your room is in there. I'll take the other room. Unless you want to trade."

"No, this is fine."

"You have a private office there, the bathroom is there, the kitchen is there, and the big room next to it is for meetings. Every room has window screens, you can tune them to Earth, Luna, Mars, various space vistas, or Praxis. I recommend Praxis."

"I was planning on it."

I jumped up and down a bit, testing. "Gravity seems a little less than Earth. But we've passed through so many portals, I might have lost my Earth legs."

"We're point nine-something. They're still calculating. The orbit creates a lot of stress. Expect earthquakes. Don't worry, everything is self-sufficient. And we're not in a quake zone, so the shakes are minor."

"Good to know, thanks." I turned to him. "Thank you for everything, Kai."

"I haven't done anything yet."

"You've been honest."

He shrugged. "Okay." And then he was official Kai again. "I have to check in and get your travel schedule. You'll have a lot of meetings. Everyone wants to meet you, get to know you before the serious discussions start. They're going to tell you what they want from you. All of them. You'll have to charm them a bit if you want them to listen to your ideas."

"Thank you, but this isn't my first rodeo. You do know what a rodeo is, don't you?"

"I've seen pictures. I understand the idiom. But I don't know if you understand Praxis."

"I guess that'll be a big part of your job. Teaching me."

He ignored that. He was all business now. "You have three hours before your first meeting. I suggest a bath and a snack. If you decide on a nap, I'll wake you in time to get dressed. You don't have to dress up. We're mostly shirts, shorts, and slippers. Look in your closet, but I suggest Earth or Lunar clothes for your first meetings. You don't want to look like an over-eager tourist. You want them to see you as an arbiter."

"Good idea, thank you."

I didn't need the nap, but I took a rest break anyway. The windows were set to Praxis, so I watched the progression from summer to hot summer back to summer, then autumn and winter and on to dark winter, then winter and long spring and finally summer again. Praxis has an unstable elliptical orbit, with one end eventually stabilizing toward the sun, another few hundred years, maybe. The seasons are severe and promise to get more so. But during spring and autumn, the days would be human survivable.

Some of the plants curl up against the worst of the seasons, some of them spread seeds, lots of them. And some endure. They look like cactus. They survive. The animals are another adaptation. Some of them fatten up when they can and burrow deeper when they can't. There are roots underground that they feed on. Life is inventive. It's also messy.

And mostly dangerous.

The micro-biology of Praxis thinks humans are delicious. Some infections are mild. Others not so. Some are debilitating. Or painful. Or fatal. Or all three. Some vaccinations work. Some don't. Some are still under development. The shirtsleevers are courageous, no question.

But shirtsleeving is the goal. It will

probably take centuries, but the prize is a whole planet.

Which is why the fight is going to be long and dirty.

And why they say they want my wisdom.

Right . . .

I was having thoughts about that.

MEETINGS

The first set of meetings was with a committee of neo-natives. Shirtsleevers. Dirtsiders, the men who lived outside—on Praxis, that wasn't an insult.

There were at least ten, maybe more. We met in a conference room that was split by a wall of glass. That was more personal and direct than a video conference. By their body language, it seemed obvious that they wanted to get a sense of this arrogant outsider who was here to tell them how to set up their government.

And so, of course, after all the appropriate greetings and welcomes and assurances that they wanted my stay to be useful and productive, each of them told me what they wanted me to do instead.

I was prepared for it. This wasn't my first circus. Kai stood politely behind me, recording everything and making extensive notes on his tablet.

"Please don't forget that . . ."

"I know you have your own ideas, but here's what you need to know about . . ."

"I think you should remember that . . ."

"When you do your research, pay special attention to . . ."

"Those of us who live outside, we have to have resources . . ."

"Don't overlook the ecological . . ."

"Medical services . . ."

"What the men who live inside don't realize is . . ."

"Pay special attention to . . ."

Only one of them, a younger man, had the temerity to ask, "So what do you think we might need . . ." but he didn't get to finish his question, because three other men pushed him aside to tell me about the importance of weather-appropriate legislation.

Uh-huh.

Later, there was a similar meeting with the men who lived inside. This time, there was a buffet table, sandwiches and coffee. But the conversations were much the same.

"What the men who live outside need to understand . . ."

"Outside they have a different set of problems. In here, we have to deal with . . ."

"Some of us still have to live inside because . . ."

"The dirtsiders, they don't understand

what it takes to manage relations with . . ."

"We're growing children now. We need to talk about educational facilities . . ."

To all of them, I said, "Right now, I'm just an observer. I'm here to learn. I'm looking, I'm listening, I'm learning, and eventually if I have something useful to contribute, I will. But it's up to the men who live here to decide what kind of government will work best here."

Maybe that would be enough, but probably not. Three days of meetings, with a promise of many more. But first—

THE JOKE

"——Oompah, right?"

We were sitting alone in my suite. Lopez looked at me curiously. "Oompah?"

"It's a joke that Grandpa likes to tell."

Lopez waited.

I explained. "Three explorers who land on a planet where they encounter alien warriors, four or five meters tall and all have very large genitals. For some reason, they decide explorers have violated one of their laws and must be punished. The chief alien gives them a choice. Death or Oompah.

"The first explorer chooses Oompah and the alien warriors tell him this is a wise choice and then all the alien warriors sodomize him, but he survives. The second explorer thinks hard, but wants to survive, so he too chooses Oompah. And he too is sodomized. The third explorer says, 'I choose death.' The Alien Chief says, 'Good choice, yes. But first Oompah!'"

Lopez and Kai both stared at me. "I don't get it," Lopez said.

"Right. I should have realized. It doesn't translate, does it?"

"Oompah is supposed to be unpleasant," Kai explained. "Oh," said Lopez. He scratched his eyebrow. "And that's funny on Earth?"

"Yes," I said. "That's funny on Earth."

Lopez frowned. "Earth men." He shook his head.

"Look," I said. "Three days of meetings, three days of everyone I meet telling me how to do my job. That's not unexpected. Everyone has an opinion. Not everyone has an informed opinion, or even an intelligent opinion. Only one or two have asked me what I've noticed, what I might suggest. I've ducked those questions deliberately, because there's already enough rumors and gossip and worries about who I am and why I'm here and what I really intend and the fact is—" I stopped.

"What?" he asked.

"I'm not here to do anything at all, am I?"

Lopez sat back in his chair. "Why do you say that?"

"I'm not stupid."

"Yes. We've already established that."

"I'm not here to advise on a constitution or the structure of a possible government or anything at all. I'm here as a distraction. The people here have been arguing about all of this for decades, right?"

Lopez nodded.

"And nothing has been decided. Tempers are up everywhere. And you're looking at the possibility of a civil war. You can't risk a breakdown. You can't risk a war, the men outside fighting the men inside. That would be a disaster, the corporations would see it as an opportunity to take over. They probably already have plans for that."

"That still doesn't explain—"

"I'm not done. You and whoever else you represent, you figured that if you all had a common enemy—me—then out of that unity of resentment, you might create a conversation of commitment, something like that, right?"

Lopez looked to Kai.

Kai looked back to Lopez. "I told you he'd figure it out."

"Oh, and one more thing." I looked to Lopez. "There were others you could have chosen. Just as qualified. Maybe even better qualified. So why me? Because I have a reputation. I'm unlikable. You said it yourself. Even my friends know I don't have any friends. That was the deciding factor, wasn't it?"

"It was a factor," Lopez admitted. "But apparently, I misjudged you."

"How so?"

"You haven't pissed off anybody as much

as we'd hoped."

"You didn't tell me that was the goal."

"I didn't think I needed to. You made your point at our first meeting. And our second. And our third."

"I admit I'm tactless." I looked across to both of them. "But I'm not dishonest."

Lopez nodded. "I apologize."

Kai nodded agreement.

"Right," I said. "Accepted."

Lopez said, "We have a train going out in two days. We'll send you back—"

"Like hell you will. I'm not quitting."

"Eh?"

"You hired me to write a constitution. It doesn't matter how good a job I do if you can't sell it to the constituents. And if you don't sell it you have an even bigger problem. So let's talk about that."

ANOTHER MEETING

Lopez pulled out his phone and said something into it. Then he folded it up and placed it back in his vest pocket.

"What was that about?" I asked.

"Plan B. Or maybe Plan R. I'm sure how many plans we've gone through now. Maybe we've run out of plans." "I assume you have time for another meeting?"

"Not if it's more of the same—"

"Oh, this will definitely not be the same. Follow me."

I followed them out, down to the lobby where we boarded a shuttle and slid through a series of tunnels.

"Where are we going?"

"Not exactly sure. The system knows, but it's coded. Security."

"Security?"

"We've had some . . . unrest."

"You're just telling me this now?"

"You were supposed to be a distraction, not a solution."

We arrived at an empty station. It looked unfinished and unused. Several of the rooms were empty of furnishings. We went through one of them to what looked like a closet door. Lopez held his hand up in front of the door and it slid open.

We stepped into a doorless room that looked a lot less innocent and here again, Lopez stepped forward and raised his hand for identification. One wall slid open revealing a comfortable suite. A conference table was divided by a glass wall. Sitting on the other side were seven men. Shirtsleevers. That was why the room was divided.

I recognized Coordinator James Patrick Dolan and his husband, José Miguel Rodríguez-Chan. They looked older than their pictures. The others were familiar, but I didn't remember their names.

Lopez nodded toward the men at the table, "Coordinator Dolan, you ordered a beagle. You got a beagle."

Dolan smiled. "Apparently, we got more than a beagle. We got a true son of a bitch." He looked to me. "That's a compliment." He gestured. "Please, sit down, Arbiter. We have a lot to talk about."

I found a place opposite the Coordinator, Lopez sat to my left, Kai to my right.

"Have you eaten? We'll order dinner." He nodded to Rodríguez-Chan who picked up his tablet. Back to me. "Let me make introductions. These are the Acting Secretaries of my administration." He named each one and their assigned duties. "We've been charged with designing a permanent government for Praxis. The sooner the better, I really do not want this job."

"I can understand that. You're on the cusp of revolution, aren't you?"

"Not quite, but . . . yes." He explained. "My authority was met with cheers. For about ten minutes. Then everybody started listing what they wanted, and we didn't have the resources or the personnel or the mechanisms to grant half their demands. And any time we tried to make a change, there was always opposition. Praxians want government, they just don't want this one. There's an old saying . . . something about grabbing a tribble by the tail?"

"Tribbles don't have tails."

"Precisely. You can't hold it and you can't let go or you end up with a thousand more. Or a million. Whatever the number. Can I offer you something to drink. We might be here a while. There's water in the pitchers in front of you, but if you want something a little stronger . . ."

"Coffee would be good."

Coordinator Dolan nodded. "Coffee it shall be." Beside him, Rodríguez-Chan nodded and tapped at his tablet.

Dolan turned back to me. "So you're not quitting?"

"You've been listening to my conversations?"

"Not all of them, but enough. It turns out you're too smart for the role we wanted you to play. So . . ." He spread his hands wide. "We're open to suggestions."

"Well, my first thought would be—I mean, if you're not seeing any alignment among your people . . ." I shrugged and pointed to the glass wall that separated us. "Going back to Earth is no longer an option, is it? So you have to eat the frog in front of you."

"An interesting colloquialism. But we don't have frogs on Praxis. We have . . . other things. Not as cute. Please . . . ?"

"I can only say the same thing that Grandpa always says—"

"Grandpa?"

"Senior Arbiter Ezra Ben Howell."

"Ah yes. A very helpful consultant. And smart. He refused our offer and suggested you instead."

"Did he tell you I didn't want to come?"

"You weren't our first choice either, but here we are. So let's go to work. What is it that your grandfather always says?"

"If you can't solve the problem, change it into one you can solve."

"Go on."

"I have notes. Not a constitution. Not a draft document. Not a preliminary set of proposals, just notes. Commander Lopez, here—" He gave me a sharp look. I met his gaze. "I do research. Did you really think I wouldn't figure out who you are?"

I turned back to Dolan. "Commander Lopez said you wanted a constitution that would be immune to time and stupidity. That's what I've been working on. It's not a set of laws, it's a set of agreements. The people, all the people, have to be signatory. A society needs a citizenry committed to maintaining the services of the government. Even if the government is flawed by the inefficiencies of human behavior. But if the services are being delivered, you have something that approaches stability.

"So that's where I started. I built on that idea. What agreements would be advantageous to a person—so advantageous that he would commit to them? It would have to be the kind of personal commitment where the individual sees his participation in the agreements as an extension of his identity. It has worked in homogenous communities. I don't know that it will work for the situations you have here on Praxis. You have two separated populations. And each of those populations is further divided. How long do your meetings last? And how much do you accomplish? That's the real problem. It doesn't matter what we come up with. You can't sell it. Nobody can. Not unless—"

"I don't know. It might be too late. What's my reputation here?"

"You're the pro from Dover."

"I don't get the reference."

"It's older than tribbles. It means you're the out-of-town expert."

"An assumption on your part."

"On your grandfather's as well."

"The problem with that is I'm the out-of-town expert. You need a local salesman."

"Most everyone here has already taken a position."

An idea occurred to me. I didn't like it. But I couldn't stop thinking about it.

"What?" Dolan asked.

I shook my head.

"Tell me anyway."

"How's your popularity?"

"Tenuous. Maybe."

"Not true," said Rodríguez-Chan next to him. "The people still admire and respect you. You stood up for them. They know where your heart is. They're looking to you for direction."

Dolan looked embarrassed. He said to his husband, "You're supposed to tell me the truth."

"I just did," José replied.

Dolan rolled his eyes. He turned back to me. "All right, go on."

"A public relations tour. Visit as many stations as you can. And at each one, ask for input. It doesn't matter what they tell you. Listen, take notes. Don't agree, don't disagree. Say it's a fact-finding tour. Find a sincere way to say, 'Thank you for sharing that' so that everybody thinks they're part of the solution. That'll buy you some time."

"And then what?"

"And then I hope one of us will have an idea what to do next."

DOLAN

The Coordinator turned to the other people sitting on his side of the table. "Let's go to the south stations. I've never been there, so it's a fact-finding visit. I want to know what they're thinking. If the response is good, we'll expand the schedule to the west, then the north and east. We'll have to be quick about it. We're heading into Autumn and then Long Winter. How many stations can we visit before we have to go deep?"

"I'll get right on it," said one of the men, the secretary of something-or-other. Transportation? Interior? I think his name was Alec something. I'd have to check with Kai. He was taking extensive notes. Rodríguez-Chan picked up his tablet. "I'll arrange transport."

Abruptly, Dolan turned back to me. He looked at me through the glass wall. His expression was stern. "You're coming with."

"Beg pardon?"

"We're going to get our money's worth out of you, one way or the other." He turned to the others. "We'll need a sealed environment for the Arbiter, and suits, and all the usual. Lopez and Kai as well. Let's make it big." Then back to me. "It's a shame that you're not emigrating. I could sell that—oh, well. We'll work around it. You're here at my request, at the committee's request. That's not a lie. And you're very impressed at what you're seeing, you think there's real possibilities here—" He looked at me suddenly. "What?"

"I'm sorry, was my face getting too loud?"

"You were smiling. What's so amusing?"

"You're very good at this."

He paused. "Did you just call me a politician?"

"I believe I did."

"I'll forgive you, this time. Don't do it again."

"If you'll stop calling me a beagle, yes."

"Deal. Now, tell me what you're thinking. Even if you're wrong, it's still a starting place."

I took a breath. I steepled my hands in front me while I considered where to begin. Beside me, Kai poured coffee. He pushed a cup in front of me. I studied it for a moment, considering what I should say. Finally, I looked up and across to Coordinator Dolan.

"To be honest, sir—I've spent too much time on Luna dealing with people who shouldn't be allowed out in public without a leash. That's not Praxis. You have engineers here. You have biologists. You have astronomers and mechanics and ecologists and scientists of all flavors. You don't have stupid people here. Opinionated? Yes. But the great majority of your people, the ones I've met, they have informed opinions. Very informed. I feel outclassed and outnumbered. And I admit to feeling that there's more than enough intelligence here that all of you should have been able to sort this all out for yourselves." I wasn't sure what to say next, so I sipped at my coffee. It was still too hot.

Dolan nodded thoughtfully. "Thank you for your candor. It's appreciated. And yes, there is more than enough intelligence here, just not the right kind. You have legal experience. Most of us don't. You have the training, the background, the history, the experience. But most of all, what I hope for, is that you also have extensive knowledge of the pitfalls, all the things that don't work. We can suggest things. We have ideas. But we don't have the background that you have." He leaned across the table toward me, his face almost inches from the glass. "I know what you've said about there being two kinds of government, control or service. We have to create a service government here, because if we don't . . ."

"I know. Corporate takeover."

KAI

The meeting lasted late. There was a lot to go through. Schedules, manifests, speeches, declarations, rough drafts, rewrites, suggestions, demands, arguments, discussions, more demands, some refusals, a few compromises and ultimately, even a consensus, followed by a few smiles and thanks. The usual.

—Until finally, Rodríguez-Chan looked up from his tablet. "The first leg of the tour is arranged. We leave in four hours."

Dolan looked to us. "Go pack. Take a shower and a nap. Set an alarm. Don't be late."

We went back to the suite, Kai checked his mail, frowned, and went to his room without saying good night.

I started for mine, then stopped. Something was wrong. I went after Kai. "Okay, what is it? And don't say nothing. I'm a lawyer. If I had you on the stand, I'd ask the judge for permission to be hostile."

He whirled to face me. "I've been drafted."

"Huh? They can't draft you—"

"They can and they did. And I know why they did. It's because I've been working with you."

"Wait a minute. Slow down. Who's they?"

"The Labor Assignments. Remember I told you, I was supposed to go shirtsleeve? That was so my family could never drag me back. Yeah, I found out they had some kind of paperwork, they were going to reregister my indenture. So I applied for outside. I was already training to go out when Lopez requisitioned me because I had Earth experience and he needed someone to report on you, and my name popped up and I was available, I didn't want to, but why not? One last adventure? So okay, I could do that, and . . . once I saw how good you are at figuring things out, I actually began to . . ." He finished the sentence with a shrug, a convenient way of avoiding having to say it. "But I still had a contract to go shirtsleeve and they just invoked it. They want to know what I know and they want to make it harder for you to do whatever it is you're going to do, and—"

"And you don't want to go?"

He looked up at me. He was just this short of crying. His eyes were filling with tears. "You're about to make history. I want to be a part of it. But now I can't."

"We're about to make history," I corrected.

121

"Um, isn't there any way I can or Lopez can or even the Coordinator can do something?"

"I don't know what it's like on Earth or Luna, but contracts mean something here."

"They mean something there too." I scratched my head. "There's always a loophole. Can I see the boilerplate?"

He went to his desk and brought his tablet back to me. "Mm," I said. I scrolled through the text. "This is pretty good. Whoever wrote it is a nasty piece of . . . work. Oh—"

"What?"

I thought for a moment. I put the tablet aside. Not a good idea. On the other hand. But maybe. I took a deep breath. It would work. I looked over at Kai. "Do you really want to stay with me?"

He nodded slowly. "This is the first time I've ever been a part of something important."

"Well, you are. More than you know." I rubbed my chin and thought some more. "When do you have to report?"

"Immediately," he said. "Like right now."

"They didn't waste any time, did they?"

"I wasn't supposed to tell you, but there's a lot of opposition here."

"The corporations?"

Kai nodded. "They fight dirty. They send memos. They invoke regulations. They make suggestions. But they never do it in person, so there's nobody to confront. Everything looks very proper and official. Until you put the pieces together and see the whole pattern of interference. They monitor everything. They probably knew that Coordinator Dolan was planning a trip as soon as he ordered the train." He held up his tablet. "This is their response." Kai looked like he wanted to scream. He looked like he wanted to cry. He looked like he wanted to be held. He looked trapped.

"Kai," I said. "You don't have to go—"

"You don't understand, there are penalties. I could even be deported back to my family. That's how these people work. Maybe they're even the ones who let my family know I'm here."

"Kai," I said. "I need you."

He stiffened. He shook his head. "I appreciate your . . . whatever. Courage. But there's nothing you can do. I have to get my things." He reached past me and picked up the little Martian. He handed it to me. "I never did thank you for him, did I? I named him Herbert. Nobody ever gave me a Martian before."

I put Herbert aside. "You're not going."

"I'm not going to break the law."

"No, you're not." I pointed. "Sit down."

He sat.

I sat opposite him. "I'm going to say something that I never thought I'd say to anyone, least of all another man. But—oh, hell. Kai, marry me."

"What?"

"Marry me!" I was still holding his tablet. I held it out for him to see. "The only contract that supersedes this one is the marriage contract. Marry me and they can't have you. No one can. Not your family, not the Labor Corps. You'll be free. No more strings."

"I don't . . . love you," he said. "And I'm not —"

"Neither am I. And I don't love you either. But marriage doesn't have to be about love. Or sex. It only has to be about partnership. And I think we're pretty good at being partners. If you think so too, say yes. And if you don't think so, then okay—go outside."

He rubbed his chin, his cheek, his forehead, even his curly dark hair. He shook his head. He frowned. He looked at the ceiling. Finally, he looked to me. "You mean it?"

"How many times do I have to say it?"

"This isn't the marriage I thought I'd have —"

"What kind of marriage were you planning?"

"I dunno. I thought maybe I'd work for a while, figure out where I wanted to settle, maybe finally rechannel and meet someone and . . . I dunno, I wasn't thinking about—" He looked at me. "Are you sure about this?"

"I'm a lawyer. I know how contracts work."

"No. I meant. This. Us." He pointed back and forth. Me and him.

I threw the question back at him. "Do you want to do this or not?"

"I think . . . yes," he said.

"Thank you. Do you want to hug or something?"

He stepped reluctantly into my arms. We held each other for a bit, then separated. He picked up his tablet where I'd dropped it. "We have to register as partners immediately. That won't be a problem. We can claim common-law partners since Luna, or maybe Mars, since Olympus Mons, that's more logical, and—oh, I have an idea. We'll ask Coordinator Dolan to perform the public vows. Nobody will dare contest it."

"He'll do that?"

"He says that's the only part of the job he likes."

So that's how I ended up with a husband.

And Herbert.

MARRIED

Getting married on Praxis starts with a conversation. Because everything starts with a conversation. But it's not real until the conversation becomes a contract.

The marriage contract is an agreement between partners specifying rights and responsibilities. But with marriage—there are also expectations, and there are as many expectations as there are people talking about marriage, whether they're married or not, but probably more expectations among those who are not married. That might be worth a research project. For someone else, not me.

What they teach in law school is that the contract of marriage is a lot like the contract for a duel. Both parties have to agree to the terms before the rest of the argument begins.

For Kai and I, it meant logging onto the Partnership Registry, filling out the forms, checking the appropriate boxes, and finally signing, thumbprinting, and having our pictures taken. Then we waited a few seconds while the intelligence engine checked that both of us were eligible and free of any legal entanglements that would invalidate the request for alliance. There were none and all of the lesser and conflicting claims on Kai were immediately suspended, with a three-year term of suspension before dissolution. It didn't mean he was free of obligation, it just meant that his partner, me, was now accepting mutual accountability. There was no financial part—and even if there had been, I suspect Lopez knew how to make it go away. The laws in this place were a slumgullion stew of whatever anyone had thrown into the pot when they arrived.

The screen announced, "The certificate of partnership has been filed. Your relationship is hereby recognized as a civil contract and is legally binding on all parties."

"How very romantic," I said.

"That was sarcasm, right?" Kai said dryly.

I looked at him. He was smiling.

"Yes," I admitted. "That was sarcasm. Where I come from, there's usually some hugging and kissing."

"Hugging? Kissing? Okay, if you insist." He stepped close to me and wrapped his arms around me. "Here's the hug." He held me tight for a moment, then took a half step back so he could look me in the eyes. "And here's the kiss."

After a bit, he pulled back. "You're supposed to kiss back."

"You surprised me."

"Excuse me?" he said.

I met his gaze. "Where I grew up, men didn't—"

"Well, here on Praxis, men do. But if you don't want to—"

I grabbed him and kissed him.

When we finally broke apart, he looked at me serious. "That's better," he said.

"Good enough?"

"It's a start."

I hesitated. "You've kissed a lot of men?"

"A few. You?"

"You're the first." I let go of him. "You've kissed others?"

He looked confused. "It's a cultural thing," he explained. "People kiss. But not everybody is cultural. Don't worry about it. You don't have to be if you don't want to."

"I'm from Earth. Luna actually. Earth's back yard."

"I know who you are and I know why you're here. I get it. This is a marriage of convenience. I won't make any demands on you. Certainly not romantic. We'll carry on as before. I assume that's what you want. The kiss was just to seal the deal, okay?"

"Um, okay." I wasn't sure how I felt about that. Disappointed or relieved. "Whatever you want."

He didn't answer. He picked up his tablet. "I'll send out the notifications."

KISSES

Coordinator Dolan came online almost immediately.

"Well, that was a surprise. I did not expect it. Congratulations to both of you. How did you convince him to say yes?"

Before I could answer, Kai spoke up. "I took off my pants." I stared at him, confused at his joke—

Dolan laughed. "I did not need that picture in my head, but . . . never mind, it's a nice picture."

And then I realized I wasn't as embarrassed as I should have been. Conversations on Praxis were a lot more . . . uninhibited. Maybe that was a good thing. Sociopaths don't tell jokes. They don't get jokes. They only know cruelty. This is how an arbiter knows which side is wrong.

Dolan turned to me. "This changes the narrative—for the better. You're not the pro from

Dover anymore. You're an immigrant. You met Kai on Luna. The two of you connected. You came here to get married. Yes, I know about the contracts, it doesn't matter. You two are a love story. Everyone loves a love story. And this makes you someone who wants to be a part of our world. We can sell this. Sorry to put it in those terms, but . . ." He shrugged. "We have a narrative to create. We have to use everything I can. And yes, of course, I'll officiate the vows. We'll do it at Kissing Rocks. Congratulations again, Kai, Dar."

He logged off and I turned to Kai. "He used my first name."

"He respects you. And he likes you."

"I got that." I looked at him curiously. "You made a joke."

"We got married."

"Yes, I was there."

"We need to act like it." he said. "If people start thinking this is a political marriage, it won't work."

"Um, okay. I guess we should at least hold hands in public. If that's all right with you."

He gave me a look. "We got married."

"Yes, you said that."

"I expect you to honor the contract."

"Of course. I don't want to get sued for breach."

Kai looked at me. "Is there a name for what's wrong with you?" He left the room.

I said, "Arbiter," but he had already closed the door behind him.

After a moment, he came back out. "I'm sorry," he said.

"For what?"

"For having expectations."

"Um . . . expectations are normal."

"But you're not."

"Excuse me?"

"Well, for one thing, you're from Earth, you're an arbiter, and . . ."

"And . . . ?"

"You're on the spectrum, aren't you?"

"That's a very old-fashioned way of saying it."

"But you are," he accused.

"Well, yes. And no."

"No?"

"I'm not neuro-atypical, because there's no such thing as neuro-atypical. All of us, we are all just points on a 93-dimension array."

"Huh?"

"There's no such thing as normal. There are only degrees of difference, in multiple directions. Some of it is noticeable as quirks or idiosyncrasies or . . . well, weirdness. I'm weird. I know it. I'm weird in a specific direction. It's an asset. So what's your point?"

Kai considered it for a long moment. "Okay, fine. But your particular direction—"

"What?"

He hesitated.

Something I learned to say in court. Something Grandpa said sometimes. "Spit it out. Before it burns a hole in your tongue."

"Sometimes, your particular direction is off toward asshole."

"If you mean, I'm not good with people, you're right. That's why I'm good as an arbiter."

"I mean you're terrible at affection."

I started to retort, then stopped myself. Momentarily speechless. He was right. But there was something else—

"Go ahead," he prompted. "Now it's your turn to say it."

"Are you saying that . . . you like me?"

"It's a dirty job, but someone has to do it."

Did he mean that as a joke? Or what? Wait —

Oh.

"What?" he demanded.

"Um . . . I like you too. That's what you wanted—needed?—to hear, right?"

He rolled his eyes. "Never mind." And then he said, "Oh, the hell with it," and grabbed me again in a hug. A ferociously tight hug. He started to say. "It's okay. You don't have to kiss me —"

He didn't get to finish the sentence.

KISSING

The thing about kissing—
—is that I don't know much about kissing.

Maybe that's why my previous attempts at relationships hadn't worked.

From a biological point of view, kissing is mostly a mechanical act, the pressing together of lips and sometimes tongues, intended as a positive affirmation of an affectional bond, as well as an additional exchange of microbial ecologies.

But kissing is also supposed to be a pleasurable experience for the participants—and in a relationship, it's an affirmation of intimacy. Physical intimacy.

Oh.

Well, that explains a lot.

Not about kissing. About me.

I don't do intimacy. I never have.

Intimacy—is vulnerability.

And vulnerability is surrender.

I don't surrender.

Maybe there's a different definition for surrender. Surrender to the relationship? Surrender to the possibility? Surrender to intimacy? No, wait—that's circular reasoning.

I closed the site and leaned back in my chair.

Maybe that's why Kai was so often annoyed with me. I'm too logical.

What was an asset in chambers was not necessarily an asset in the bedroom.

There's no logic to affection.

No, that's not right.

There's a whole other kind of logic. Non-Aristotelian. Except maybe, very Aristotelian. Who did that old geezer sleep with anyway? And why? History doesn't say much about that.

I looked at my coffee cup. It was almost empty. According to the temperature gauge on the side, the little bit that remained was cold. Ordinarily, I'd have asked Kai to get me a refill, but . . . no.

Instead, I took the cup to the kitchen, rinsed it out, then punched for a refill.

Kai came up beside me. "I could have done that for you."

I shook my head. "We're partners now. Do you want coffee?"

"No time. We have to leave in a few minutes."

I handed him the cup. "Share this with me?"

He took it in both hands, sipped, looked at me. "Are you all right?"

"I've been thinking about what you said."

He waited for me to continue.

"It's about context."

"?"

"We can't pretend in public and be apart in private. It won't work. It's what you said. People will see it. We have to be married everywhere. In here, we'll practice. I'll practice. You'll help me."

"Is this your way of admitting you're an asshole?" Kai said it with a smile.

"Well, at the moment, I'm your asshole. So deal with it."

He handed me back the cup. "It's time to go."

We told the luggage to follow us and headed out to the pod station.

We would get to the first settlements by train, but for the rest of the tour, we would travel by pod-trucks or flyers. Praxis hadn't bought enough vacuum balls to build a proper airship, and the weather here was too dangerous for dirigibles, but the flyers were weight-balanced, not quite crash-proof, but survivable.

Once aboard the train, Kai logged us in and began sending out official notices to all concerned parties that their contracts had been superseded and were now null and void, for at least three years, possibly longer. According to current Praxis law, we had to stay together at least three years or the contract-holders could reapply. I wondered if Kai would want to return to Luna with me when my service was complete. Probably not. Oh well.

Grandpa sent me an angry note. "I expected you to write a goddamn constitution, not go native. Don't you dare go shirtsleeve!"

I showed it to Kai. He smiled. "Your family. Mine. They should marry each other."

"I'm not sure who would survive that. Grandpa eats human flesh."

"Grandma did too."

"Sounds like a match made in Hell."

Kai reached over and held my hand for a bit. "Thank you," he said.

"No, I should thank you. I've never seen Grandpa so angry."

He squeezed my hand, then turned back to his tablet. And I sat staring out the screen that pretended it was a window, wondering what I was feeling.

PANGAS

After a while, we went to bed.

Kai fell asleep quickly. He lay next to me, snoring softly. I stared at the bulkhead above and wondered what I'd done. This wasn't me. Not the me I used to be. So if I wasn't who I used to be, who was I now?

What if Kai wanted to rechannel? Would he want me to rechannel? Would I? What would that be like? I didn't have anything against it. Not exactly. But always before it had been a hypothetical. Like skydiving. I wasn't planning on that either.

Technically, the process was simple, and it didn't change a person's orientation. It just shifted the affectional bias, expanding it to include a wider range of emotional possibility. That's what the documentation said. Essentially, it was about expanding a person's ability to be empathic, making it easier to connect to others, making partnership, intimate and otherwise, more likely. And yes, it could, but not necessarily, allow for an increase in same-sex attraction. But that was not the primary purpose. Technically.

But I'd heard—I'd been told that rechanneling was transformative, enlightening, and that the sex was better. There was considerable discussion about that. Was it actually true or was it something that rechanneling made you believe? There had been years of research, studies, tests, and testimonials. And a person could always channel back, so the change wasn't necessarily permanent, but very few people channeled backward. Therefore, rechanneling was statistically permanent.

At the moment, it was also statistically hypothetical. Kai didn't love me. I didn't love him. This was strictly a professional arrangement and at the end of my term, we could part. If he wanted to. If I wanted to. If we wanted to. But if I didn't care for him on some level, why did I marry him?

Somewhere in that tangle of thought, I must have fallen asleep. When I awoke, sunlight was streaming in through the windows—through the displays. Kai came out of the shower, a towel wrapped around his waist. "You're up? I'll order breakfast. You have messages."

"Urgent?"

"After you eat."

"Thank you." I made my way to the

shower. Having a husband to help out was a good idea. Hell, if it annoyed Grandpa, it was a great idea.

Southward, we rolled through dark forest. The trees had thick trunks and shaggy layers of furry black bark. They looked like the legs of giant animals. Above us, the sheltering canopy was so thick that only the occasional beam of blue sunlight illuminated the motes in the air. All the pods had their exterior lights on and we moved through a sparkling purple cloud.

"It must have been quite a job carving a track through this tangle."

Kai shook his head. "Before my time. I heard they followed one of the animal trails. This track is elevated so it won't interfere with the migrations, but the herds have carved a lot of paths through here. The trees depend on their droppings.

"What kind of herds? I haven't seen any big animals."

"Pangas. They're flightless birds. They can flap, they can glide a short way, but only when the winds are strong enough. They're solitary in summer. That's when they fatten up. They don't eat in winter. When they start forming herds, it's a warning. Cold weather is coming. We might see them out on the plains. Some of the herds shelter in this forest. This time of year, they're starting to gather."

"You know a lot about the ecology?"

"If you want to go shirtsleeve, you have to."

"Yeah, that makes sense."

He pointed to my screen. "The new constitution?"

"Not a constitution. Notes."

"Uh-huh." He peered close. "Nice preamble."

"Do you want to see my articles too?"

He blinked. "Are you flirting with me?"

"I don't know. Am I?"

"You know . . ."

"What?"

"You're better at this than you think."

"I have a reason to."

"Ooh, a compliment, I'll take it."

"If that'll get me a cup of coffee, I'll do it again."

"I should have known there was a catch. Black as your heart, right?"

He ducked into the kitchen and I leaned back in my chair, realizing something.

Back on Luna, almost all of the cases I'd heard were negative, people acting badly toward each other. Only occasionally did I get to feel good about being an arbiter. The only exception was the half dozen marriages I'd performed—and only two of those couples were still married.

Here on Praxis, I was part of something important, something positive. And it wouldn't be just the originating document, there would be years of rulings to establish precedents. If I could end up on the Supreme Court here, I could argue that the intention of the Constitution was service to the population. If the courts could establish service as a guiding precedent, there might be a chance for Praxis to become the right kind of world.

Kai came back with a carafe and two mugs. He sat down opposite me. "You're smiling."

"Oh, sorry. I didn't mean to."

"No prob. It happens."

"Really? Have you ever smiled."

"I did once."

"Tell me about it."

"Yesterday. Somebody I hated proposed to me."

"That must have been tough."

"There was only one thing I could do."

"Really?"

"Yeah, I married him. So I could make him miserable too."

"I don't think that's working out."

"Yeah. I caught him looking happy."

"Oh, look—" He pointed past me. "Those are pangas."

I looked to the window. The pangas were three meters tall and looked like furry gray bowling pins with large dark eyes and long pointed snouts.

"They're cute," I said.

"The adults can be five to six meters tall.

You don't want to go near them. They're nasty things. And I'm told they smell bad. Like rancid fat. The weather is turning, I see at least twenty, maybe thirty. They're getting ready to form a herd. And when the snow starts falling, they cluster. They need the biggest cluster possible to survive. Have you seen the videos?"

I shook my head.

"They've been studying the pangas for decades, trying to figure out how they survive dark winter. The adult pangas inside rotate to the outside and the outside ones rotate inside. They all keep rotating and that's how they keep the interior of the cluster warm enough so the whole group survives."

"Makes sense. Survival of the whole community."

"You should see the overhead videos. A small cluster rotates like a pinwheel, with the outside ones moving inward and the inside ones moving outward, but the bigger clusters have multiple interior rotations, like a set of interlocked gears. The bigger the cluster, the more individuals can keep warm enough to survive. The goal is a mega-cluster. At the very inside, they'll generate enough heat to keep the eggs warm enough to hatch. The eggs start to hatch in the Spring when grazing is available again. The adults have to live off their fat all winter, so the summer is about fattening up. Did you know they have three sexes? Sperm producer, egg producer, and egg-carrier."

"Mm."

"What?"

"I have a hard enough time finding a date with two sexes."

"You're through dating," Kai said. "You're married."

"To a man."

"Well . . . nobody's perfect."

I watched the screens for a while, thinking about Praxis and pangas and clusters. "I heard that when they cluster, that's when the adults mate, is that right?"

Kai looked at me, one eyebrow raised. "Yes, it's a cluster-fuck. That's one of the things you people think is funny."

"'You people?'"

"Earth people."

"I'm not an Earth people. Not anymore."

"But you're not a Praxian. Not really."

I didn't have an answer for that. Not yet. I wasn't sure who I was. I half-raised my hand. I had something to say.

"What?"

"I was thinking about what you said. About the pangas. It's like our situation."

"Our?" He looked confused. "You and me? Or—?

"Yes, I said 'our.' I meant all of us. And you and me."

He waited for me to explain.

"It's a metaphor. Maybe our political situation is a cluster-fuck, but it's also an opportunity. The more we take care of each other, the better it is for all of us. Survival is a group effort. Everybody does their part. You and me too."

Kai didn't answer immediately. Apparently, this was one of those conversations, interrupted by long thoughtful pauses. Finally, he said, "You're not the first person to make that observation."

"Who was the first?"

"Coordinator Dolan. His first trip outside."

"Oh."

KISSING ROCKS

José Rodríguez-Chan liked to organize things. He organized our wedding. He also made sure the ceremony would be streamed everywhere. We were news.

He also ordered the rings. I hadn't thought about rings. I don't wear jewelry, only a single phone-button in my right ear. So Kai asked him to be his best man and I asked Lopez to be mine.

We arrived at Kissing Rocks mid-morning. The sky was the brightest blue I'd ever seen. In the distance, behind the dark mountains, gray clouds edged with purple piled up high, not yet warning of future storms, but hinting at the possibility.

The Kissing Rocks are two very large boulders, sitting alone on a rocky plain, not quite the same, one larger than the other, but both sort of egg-shaped with their pointed ends just touching each other. They were a local landmark, a tourist destination.

It was traditional for romantic couples to get photographed kissing beneath the granite osculation. So that's where Coordinator Dolan had us perform our vows.

The only problem was that we weren't shirtsleevers.

We had a choice. Kai and I would ride the short distance from the train to the Kissing Rocks in a transparent micro-pod. This was sort of traditional. When and if we ever became shirtsleevers, we could take the picture naked—without bio-suits. Or actually naked. That was a tradition too.

Coordinator Dolan wore his ceremonial robe, so there would be no doubt this was an official act. José Rodríguez-Chan and the other attendants wore simpler robes, but also ceremonial. They walked up the slope to the Kissing Rocks, turned to face us, and waited for the micro-pod to arrive in place. Lopez managed the micro-pod. He walked behind it in a bio-suit.

Kai and I had decided to wear plain white longshirts and shorts, as simple as possible. I don't like pretention and Kai agreed that anything more might reek of privilege. We had to avoid even the appearance of arrogance.

We held hands and faced Coordinator Dolan through the glass.

"Do you have rings?"

I nodded. We had the rings inside the pod with us. I opened the case and put it on the table in front of us.

Coordinator Dolan faced Kai first.

"Do you, Kai, give yourself, freely and completely to a partnership with . . . ?"

"I do."

Dolan turned to me. "Do you, Dar, give yourself, freely and completely to a partnership with . . . ?"

"Yes, I do."

He looked to me, he looked to Kai. We both picked up rings. "Right. Repeat after me. With this ring, I thee wed—"

I looked at Kai. He looked at me. Our eyes met. And we froze in the moment. Expectant. This was it. I felt a rush of fear, as if I stood on the edge of a chasm. Waiting to leap. Kai looked at me expectantly.

I took his hand in mine and somehow found the words. "With this ring, I thee wed." I slid the ring onto the first finger of his right hand.

He took my hand then. "With this ring, I thee wed." And slid the matching ring onto the first finger of my right hand.

Outside the pod, Dolan grinned his approval. "This partnership is now sanctified in the eyes of men and it is my privilege to pronounce you married. You do not need my permission to kiss your husband—"

Kai's eyes were shining. He leaned into my embrace and kissed me. I kissed him back.

Afterward I said, "Did I do that right?"

Kai said, "We should practice."

"If you insist."

I pulled him to me—

When I finally let go, Kai blinked. "Okay, that should convince everyone. It convinced me."

Before I could say anything, Lopez rapped on the glass. "If you two are through consummating—or is there more?—we're ready to go."

Kai looked at me, hopefully. "Is there more?"

I looked to Lopez. "There's more." I turned back to Kai—

When we paused for breath, I said. "I have a question for you."

"The answer is yes."

"I think you should wait until I ask it."

"I know what you're going to ask. The answer is yes."

"Okay. What am I going to ask?"

"If I want peach-filled crepes for lunch. Yes, I do."

"Me too, but no, that wasn't the question."

"Oh, the other one? Yes, if you want to rechannel, I do too. If you want to."

Before I could answer—

THE QUAKE

The news services called it a quake. But it wasn't. Somewhere below the horizon, something happened and something trembled and far beneath us, something slipped. The shock waves rolled across the land.

The rocks above us wobbled.

There's something Grandpa used to say. He spoke from his experiences during the revolution. I loved those stories when I was young, but not after I realized that adventures are dangerous—that's what makes them adventures. Injuries are traumatic, pain is debilitating, and death is permanent. You don't get resurrected for the sequel.

What Grandpa pointed out is that violence is the first word of the incompetent. The competent try everything else first. This is important to know—because if the enemy goes to violence early, they're admitting their intellectual deficit.

But . . . just the same, the intention of violence is always deadly.

Coordinator Dolan and José Rodríguez-Chan looked to each other, then walked determinedly downhill, followed by their attendants. There was no way he was going to be photographed running.

Portal-Master Lopez was in charge of the micro-pod. He steered us quickly downhill.

Fortunately for everyone, the Kissing Rocks toppled away from us. The ground trembled. Clouds of yellow dust rose into the air. It left us all shaken, but nobody was hurt. And the photographers got some great shots for the midday newscasts.

Kai and I transferred back to our pod in the train. I sat trembling until Kai brought me tea. He was uncommonly calm. "How can you be so . . . so . . . ? We could have been killed."

"We were never in any danger."

"How do you know that?"

He didn't answer. He nodded toward the hatch. Lopez had sterile-showered in the airlock. He peeled off his bio-suit and came into our compartment.

Kai tapped a screen to life so we could see Coordinator Dolan making a statement to the media. "Yes, this is a quake zone, that's why we don't build here. Fortunately, nobody was hurt. It's amazing those rocks lasted as long as they did. . . ."

Lopez watched, frowning. He shook his head. "Whoever triggered this, they were incompetent. And stupid. They destroyed a beloved landmark. Right there, they didn't win any friends." He paused, then added, "But the other mistake was the big one. If' you're going to shoot at someone, you'd better get them with the first shot. If you don't, you're just going to make them angry. Angry enough to shoot back."

He shook his head again, then turned to me. "Are you all right?" He looked to Kai. "And you?"

Kai said, "We're a little shaken up. We should have expected it."

Lopez said, "We did."

"Huh?" That was me. I put my cup of tea down.

"I can't tell you how we knew. I don't even know myself. But we knew they were going to try something. Those rocks, The way they were situated, they were supposed to fall this way and crush us. Specifically, Coordinator Dolan. But you would have been the gravy."

Kai looked at him. "Better tell him the rest."

"You can."

The man I had just married turned to me and said, "After you proposed, after Coordinator Dolan agreed to perform the ceremony, Commander Lopez came out with a small crew and hammered shims under the rocks. On this side. There was no way they could have fallen toward us. I would have gone with them, but the Commander here wanted me to stay with you. In case they tried anything more direct—"

"Wait. Are you saying—"

"Lopez told you. I'm your bodyguard."

I thought about that for a moment. "But that was just—no, wait. Why am I a target?"

"You're dangerous. You're the guy who knows how to turn the whole basket over."

Lopez said, "After today, I think we're all targets." He looked directly to me. "We represent independence. Independence is always dangerous. At least now we know how desperate they are to stop us."

I put my head in my hands. I leaned forward to keep myself from throwing up. "This is . . . I just wanted to . . ." I looked to Lopez. "You should have told me this—"

"You were looking for a reason to quit. This would have been it."

I thought about it. "No. I've been threatened before. I would have accepted the challenge."

"I couldn't take the chance."

I stood up, pulled up my longshirt and turned around. "Is my backbone still there?"

Lopez patted me on the back and pulled my shirt back down. "At the time, I wasn't sure. My apologies. I underestimated you."

"Don't do it again. I want honesty. From both of you." I looked to Kai. "Especially you. Especially now."

Kai looked to Lopez. "As you can see, there's been a shift in my priorities. I belong to my husband now."

"Thank you," I said. "Now tell me, who are we up against? Are there names?"

"We have suspects. No hard evidence. They're very good at that. But then, the corporations have been doing this since . . . I dunno, at least since that asshole Columbus tried to cheat the government of Spain." He added, "You shouldn't be surprised. You said it yourself enough times on Luna. Follow the money. The bigger the crime, the more likely the motive is money. Even war is a clash of economies."

He was right. Well, of course. He was quoting me. I sat down again. "I should have expected something, yes. I must have been distracted."

"Well, I am adorable," Kai said. He grinned at me.

I looked up, annoyed. "Please don't do that."

"Do what?

"I'm not used to being flirted with. Not by a man."

He shrugged. "You're my husband now. Deal with it."

Deal with it. Yes. I allowed myself a smile.

"You're really enjoying this, aren't you?"

"I like watching the expressions you make. I worry that one day, you'll start to like me flirting and I'll have to find something else to embarrass you."

Lopez interrupted then. "There's a bottle of champagne in the fridge. Do you want to open it?"

"Huh?"

"You just got married. I think you're entitled to celebrate."

"Oh, right."

Kai nodded his agreement and went to the galley. I sat back in my chair, feeling very strange. Mostly uneasy. But also . . . weird.

BLUE LIGHT

Of course, the conspiracy theorists pounced on the moment. The seismographic record of the quake's epicenter was atypical. There was no fault line there, only a dormant fracture. Therefore, there had to be a human agency involved. Or space aliens. Or ghosts. Maybe the corporation, but their spokesmen laughed at the idea, which was all the more suspicious.

And so on.

Praxis circles a blue star. It has an official name, but the Praxians call it Uncle Daddy. I'm not sure why, there are multiple histories, all of them contradictory.

Uncle Daddy paints the terrain with a shifted color palette. Instead of yellow, things are green. Instead of green, turquoise. Shadows are purple. Trees are dark and sinister. But sometimes there are gossamer webs of nearly transparent pink and white hanging from the branches.

Humans do not do well with blue light, we've evolved under yellow light, so most of the shirtsleevers wear orange goggles if they have to spend any time in the sun. But for people like me, the chance to see Praxis as it really is—it's a reminder that I'm not in Kansas anymore. This is a truly alien place. Well, I never was in Kansas, but I've seen pictures. It's all sepia toned, right?

There is this, it's a lot harder to get a sunburn on Praxis.

We rolled across a plain of bright blue grass for an hour or two, giving Kai and I a chance to talk.

"You really don't like flirting?" he asked.

"In private, it's okay."

"Okay. Can I sit with you?"

"Please." He parked himself on the couch next to me.

"May I kiss you?"

"As you wish—"

He stopped himself just long enough to acknowledge the reference.

Afterward, he looked at me, slightly puzzled. "I think I figured something out. About you."

I waited.

"The way you kiss."

"What?"

"Like you're scared to kiss. I mean, you do kiss. But there's always a hesitation at first."

"Luna," I said. "Earth."

He cocked an eye at me. "They don't kiss?"

"No, they do. But where I come from, kissing is . . . it's a prelude."

"Oh." He thought about it. He shook his head. "Not here. Kissing is just . . . kissing."

"I'm starting to get that."

"I like kissing you," he said.

"Even with my hesitation?"

"It's part of the charm." He leaned in close. It was charming.

Afterward, I said, "I've been thinking."

"Uh-huh?"

"If it's something you want, we could. . . ."

"Do you want to?"

"Umm."

"What?"

"Well . . ."

He pulled back. "Oh,"

"No, it's not that. It's . . . see, I thought I'd come here, do my job, and go home. Except . . . we're married now. Would you go with me? I don't think you'd be happy on Luna or Mars. But I don't know if I'd want to stay on Praxis. Maybe. I don't know how I'll feel in three years. About us. About Praxis. About anything. But mostly about us? Are we married? Or are we *married*?"

Kai frowned, thinking, considering. "We don't have to decide today, do we?"

"Well, we did just exchange vows."

"And times change, people change.

Relationships evolve. I used to hate you."

"The feeling was mutual."

"I was taught to trust first impressions."

"Me too."

"But here we are, married anyway.

"And kissing too."

"Don't change the subject."

"Are we flirting?"

"We will be in a minute." Kai pulled back to look me in the eye. "But right now, neither of us can predict the future. Here's my promise. When the time comes, we figure it out together. And if this turns into a forever marriage, then you will be stuck with me forever. Wherever we end up."

A sudden thought occurred to me. "I have to ask you something. And I want an honest answer."

"Yes?"

"You started out as my bodyguard, right?"

He nodded.

"Was it also part of the plan that you would marry me?"

Kai pulled back. "Damn, you're good."

"So it was?"

"No. I just meant you're good at this stuff. Seeing conspiracies. Even where there aren't any. But no. It was considered, but I said no."

"But you married me anyway."

"I changed my mind."

"Was it something I said?"

He shrugged. "Well, it seemed like a good

idea at the time."

"Are we flirting now?"

"What do you think?"

SATISFACTION

We arrived at Satisfaction.

Not its official name, of course. The official names had been designated by the Praxis Authority and it was no secret that most of the shirtsleeve population of Praxis had a low opinion of the distant bosses. They weren't here, they didn't know, they'd never come out to actually see and understand the strange beauty of this blue-tinged world. At best, the Authority was perceived as the most annoying tentacle of some distant octopoidal cartel. At worst—the locals were compiling an extensive dictionary of ways they had, and were still inventing, to describe the Authority, none of them complimentary.

So the locals invented their own names for places, usually irreverent.

And because I was suspiciously viewed as a Person From Porlock, another of their names for anyone who might be a tool of the Portal

Authority, I had to show them that I wasn't. Kai and I agreed to hold hands everywhere in public. And if he ever felt like kissing me, I promised to kiss him back. Maybe that would help. I wasn't sure what else we could do.

Satisfaction was a set of dug-in barns and tunnels in the center of a hundred acres of farms and greenhouses. The goal here was to determine what crops could be safely grown during Praxis' long summers. They'd had some luck with wheat and rye and barley, but corn was still iffy and had to be nurtured in greenhouses. Other crops included tomatoes, cucumbers, potatoes, cabbage, lettuce, carrots, peas, and various spices like garlic and basil. Some thrived, some struggled, some refused the blue sunlight. But the greenhouses were dug in deep and lit by solar lamps and those crops produced enough that Satisfaction could supply most of the other local stations with fresh vegetables and fruit. The orchards had to be indoor installations. Earth-evolved trees couldn't survive Praxis seasons.

The other problem was Praxis, which had its own predatory ecology. Some of the insects loved Earth crops, some of the wildlife too, but the worst were the microbial infestations. Kai knew more about it than I did. He shared the immediate challenges, then pointed me toward specific articles. If I looked stupid, the trip would be a disaster.

Dolan's briefings were short. "Be charming."

"Um—"

"Yes, I know. Fake it."

"Um—"

"You're a stranger. You have to show them you're not an enemy. Be interested in everything you're seeing. Be impressed. Ask intelligent questions. Nod your head a lot, even if you don't understand. And don't ask them what they want from an independent Praxis government until they start complaining about the Portal Authority. You could say, 'Well, how can we do it better?'"

"Yes, thank you."

"Oh, and one more thing. You're not an arbiter here. You're just another shlub from Earth."

"Luna."

"Same thing."

"You have no authority here, remember that. You're just a guy wants to emigrate, so you can be with your husband who you dearly love. So you want them to educate you, so you can be an asset to the community. Oh, and if they ask your opinions about anything, just say, 'I don't know enough yet. What do you suggest?' Because you really don't know anything and if you say the wrong thing, no matter how well-intentioned, we might as well not bother."

I nodded. "Thank you. Anything else?"

"Whatever they put in front of you, eat it. And say how much you like it. They're putting on their best for us. Coordinators don't visit the farms very often." He thought for a moment. "I think that should cover it. If you have any other questions, your husband should be able to answer them."

The Satisfactors, as they called themselves, were more scientists than farmers, but their various members brought experience from three worlds and Luna before they came to Praxis, but then good farming was a science. Several of them had backgrounds in gene-splicing as well.

We were given a tour of the station, then the outdoor acreage, the barns and finally the underground installations. Lopez and Kai and I followed in the micro-pod. Coordinator Dolan and his retinue walked with our hosts, chatting amiably. He sampled everything, especially the grapes, carrying a generous cluster as the tour proceeded, snacking as he went, sharing them with his husband, José.

They had been experimenting, without much success yet, cross-splicing Terran plants with Praxian. They said they were learning from their mistakes and hoped their research would literally bear fruit within the next three years.

Finally all of us returned to the station for lunch. Dolan sat with the Satisfactors. We were seated behind glass at the end of the chamber.

Our meals had to be sterilized and passed through an airlock. There wasn't anything on the plate that we didn't have from the farms at Portal City—tomatoes, cucumbers, peas, carrots, bread and butter, fried potatoes, noodles in sweet sauce, and vanilla pudding for dessert.

The servings were generous. I wasn't used to that. Food on Luna was pricey and processed—nobody wasted anything. But here? Lopez leaned over to me and whispered, "Don't eat it all."

An empty plate implied that the host had been stingy. Leaving a few bites uneaten demonstrated that they had given us more than enough to fill our bellies. But we had to eat enough to say that we had enjoyed what they served.

At the end of the meal, Dolan stood up and praised the meal, our hosts, and everything they had shown us during the tour. He then pointed toward me and apologized for my reticence. "Dar is a good friend, well-educated, eager to learn, but a bit shy when it comes to meeting new people. Apparently, he likes it here, he just married one of our local boys, so this is definitely more than a visit. Now you know I'm working on a new constitution, and I've asked him for his legal advice more than once, and he's been quite helpful—that is, when he's not saying he doesn't know enough yet. Please . . ." He waved toward me.

I stood up and bowed with my hands

steepled in front of me in a gesture of respect. "Thank you, Coordinator Dolan, for those generous words. Let me thank our hosts for the kind of meal I hope to get used to. Let me also add how impressed I am with all of the work being done here, especially the research into cross-splicing. That's remarkable. I look forward to tasting the results. I hope you'll invite me and my husband back again. Next time perhaps, we won't even need this damn micro-pod."

Dolan gave me a smile of approval and invited the Satisfactors to give me their sense of what Praxis would need for the future. "He'll take notes and report to the entire committee when we get back, so please . . ."

STARFLAKE
STATION

After Satisfaction, we rolled another three hours south and up to the top of Mount Whynot to meet with the Starflakes, that's what they called themselves. Starflake Station was the second biggest observatory on Praxis. The biggest was in the other hemisphere and we weren't going there, not this trip.

Astronomers came from Earth, Luna, and Mars, eager to study the unique situation of Praxis, the blue star, the elliptical orbit, and the dramatic skies. High-altitude vehicles had been assembled here to launch orbiting satellites.

Like all of the other portal stations, Praxis did not seem to be in any galaxy observable from Earth. So every station was an opportunity to study a unique and different galaxy.

Some of the galaxies seemed younger than

the Milky Way, some quite a bit older, and that implied that randomly opened portals were also time-windows. Nobody was willing to say for sure, not yet, but it certainly would explain why some exploratory portals opened up onto sheer black nothingness.

So Starflake Station had its share of portal engineers as well, studying the connection—it was an order of math that taxed the abilities of even an IRMA-level intelligence engine. After the third attempt to explain it to me, I shook my head and said, "Magic holes in space, right?"

"Yeah, that's accurate," they replied.

Starflake Station had its own small farm, mostly underground. It produced enough to sustain the community and even store enough for winter.

Most of the astronomers were considered tourists. They lived in contained environments and were limited to six-month tours. Then they had to leave to make room for the next man on the waiting list. But it wasn't unusual for one of them to walk out the airlock and become a shirtsleever, thereby securing a permanent position at the station. Usually, it was planned in advance so that appropriate preparations could be made, but there had been a few surprises too.

But Starflake Station was funded by the Portal Authority and some of the astronomers had close links with their funding organizations. They had very specific ideas and were eager to share them. Fair enough. Lunch wasn't meager, but it wasn't generous either. I cleaned my plate. To hell with manners.

Our next stop was Hole-In-The-Ground, a large copper mine. Giant machines had been assembled here with the intention of digging out the ore. Someday, when the mine was no longer functioning as a mine, the pit would be roofed over and a new city would be built here, so the miners considered themselves pioneers. Some were shirtsleevers, others wore bio-suits and slept and ate in containments.

The miners had their own ideas for the future of Praxis, they were a very different breed from the astronomers. These men were building their own future.

Dolan charmed them by talking enthusiastically about the city they would someday build here. I spoke about the kind of a city they might imagine—a place that included wilderness areas that wound through the entire environment, so they would never lose their connection with the rest of the world. That played well and Dolan gave me a thumbs up.

After Hole-In-The-Ground, we went to Malcolm's Folly, which was originally intended as a getaway resort for tourists who wanted to explore the Blue Mountains, but had eventually morphed into a honeymoon destination for shirtsleevers. They celebrated our marriage with a banquet, but we did not stay long enough for an appropriate consummation. That was something we had not yet negotiated anyway.

And so on. While we were rolling from one station to the next, I compiled their thoughts. Some were useful. Some were unworkable. A few were imaginative. Some were selfish, some were idealistic, some were just silly. But every so often, like a gold nugget buried under a mountain of horse exhaust, there was something insightful, something worth serious discussion with Dolan and his assistants.

Kai and I settled into a routine that was almost comfortable. One night, while lying in bed, side by side, waiting to fall asleep, he even admitted, "I'm kinda glad I married you. This is an adventure."

"Did you go off and get rechanneled without me?"

"Not yet. But I can make an appointment for the both of us. Whenever you want?"

"Are you flirting or are you serious?"

He thought about it. "Depends. What do you want? Flirting or serious?"

It was my turn to fall silent, thinking. "The thing about rechanneling..."

"Yes?"

"What if it doesn't work? I mean—"

"It always works," he said. "Even when it doesn't."

"That's what I mean."

"I don't understand."

"What if . . ."

"Just say it already."

"What if we do it and it isn't good?"

"You mean the sex?"

"Uh-huh.

"Sheesh, you are a prude. Why didn't you say that in the beginning?"

"Because, as you so accurately pointed out, I am a prude." I explained. "Living on Luna, where everything is crowded ass-to-elbow, you put up psychological walls. There's stuff you don't talk about, because it's intrusive."

"And sex is one of those things?"

"Uh-huh."

"And you came to Praxis anyway? How have you survived this long?"

"How have you put up with me this long?"

"I've been wondering about that myself." He added, "Maybe it's because you kiss good. Finally."

"Huh?"

He rolled over on his side to face me. "Kissing is both a science and art. I shall be scientific for you because you seem to be a little slow in art appreciation."

"Please. Elucidate."

"I shall. There are different kinds of kisses, each with its own specific meaning. A quick peck, for instance—" He demonstrated. "—That doesn't really mean much, does it? It says, 'I like you, we're good, see you soon.' Right?"

I nodded. "Okay."

"And then there's this. Lip to lip. Maybe a hint of an open mouth. But no tongue. Here, I'll show you—" Afterward, "Nice. A hint of intimacy, but no promises. Just a nice way to say, 'I care.' It's the familiarity of friends. That's what most kissing is. Here on Praxis, anyway."

"Can I ask you something? Have I been missing the cues? Is that a problem?"

"Yes and no. Yes. You're seen as cold and stand-offish. Like most tourists. Like most Earthers. And no, because you're married now and you're being faithful to me. Which most people can appreciate. But me especially."

"Oh, okay."

"Now, let me tell you about the third kind of kiss. It's between lovers. Sometimes married couples, but more often lovers. You and I, we've done it a couple times, but not completely. I mean, the mechanics might seem the same, but it's really about the feelings—the emotional context that motivates the kiss. Am I getting too scientific for you?"

"I think I get the point."

"Do you want to try?"

"You didn't ask me before."

"This is different. You have to really care about the person you're kissing."

I looked at him, long and hard. His eyes were shining. "Okay, let's try."

After a few moments. "How'd I do?"

"Um, I think we need to try again—"

"Is that because—"

"Shut up and kiss me."

I did. And I did.

After a moment, I said. "I think I'm getting it. Let me—"

After another moment, we pulled apart and looked at each other, a little astonished.

Kai touched my lips with gentle fingers, as if exploring the source of the connection. "If you keep doing that, I won't need rechanneling."

"I think I need a bit more convincing," I said. He rolled back into my arms.

And later, when we pulled apart, I asked, "Is there a fourth kind of kissing?"

"You're not ready for it yet." Kai said. "Neither am I—"

OTHER
POSSIBILITIES

After Martin Town, we headed north to Oh-Hell-No. Then a quick stopover at Buster before moving on to Rhee. Then Blanton and Bird and Ask-Not. The local names were a lot more interesting than the official ones. Who wanted to visit Station A5 and Station C7 and Station X2?

And then I lost track.

We were on our way from Somewhere to Nowhere, or maybe it was the other way around, Nowhere to Somewhere, and yes, those were their names, when Lopez came upstairs to talk to us. He noticed we were sitting close together, my hand resting on his leg.

"Did you guys rechannel without telling me?"

"Not yet. We're just practicing for when we

do."

"Oh, okay." He sat down opposite us. "Do you have time to talk?" He looked serious.

Kai and I exchanged a glance. I looked back to Lopez. "What's on your mind?"

"You've been passing drafts of your proposed constitution to Coordinator Dolan. He likes what he's read, so much so that he wants to publish your draft. I'm here to ask if you're ready. And if you're not, how long till you can be?"

"There are some sections I haven't finished, but give me a day or two—"

Kai put his hand on my arm. "You're ready."

"You think so?"

"Definitively."

I gave him a look. He gave it right back to me.

"Okay," I said. "Let me reread it one more time."

That should have satisfied him, but Lopez made no move to rise. "There's something else." He looked like he didn't want to say it. "We might have a problem. I don't know."

"They're planning another attack?"

"I don't know. Nobody knows. We thought we had good intelligence, but it went dark. Either they're planning something or they're not. We think they've gotten suspicious so they're not talking where we can listen."

"Are we in any danger?"

"I don't think so. Probably not. A second incident on the goodwill tour would be a tactical mistake. But—"

"But what?"

"There's chatter. Maybe it doesn't mean anything. Maybe it's just noise. Worry is worshipping the problem. Or workshopping it. Whatever. But it's my job to worry. It's my job to imagine what I would do if I were them so we can be prepared."

"And . . ."

"They're afraid we might vote for independence. According to the charter, we have that right, but only if we can prove we're self-sufficient."

"Aren't we?"

"Not yet. We have a long way to go. We still depend on downline resources. Praxis has a serious trade imbalance. We can't survive without corporate sponsorship. We were supposed to be profitable by now. We aren't. And not for a while yet. From their side, we look like a hole in space into which they pour money, with no predictable possibility of profit for at least another decade. They have shareholders—people whose long-term vision only extends as far as the next dividend."

"Then they shouldn't have invested in portals. I don't know that any of them have earned out."

"The mining stations have. But not the

settlements like Praxis where there are ecological concerns. It takes years, decades, to determine how any ecology is balanced. That's one of the reasons why Praxis has very strict controls on mining. Hole-In-The-Ground was a fight that lasted more than a decade."

I held up a hand to interrupt. "Okay, I get the context. What's the content?"

"Eh?"

"You said your job is to worry. What are you worrying about?"

"I might be wrong. I hope I'm wrong. But there are people upstairs, way upstairs, people who think in numbers, who are arguing that Praxis is getting too expensive. It's not too far from that conversation to one about cutting their losses."

"Pulling out? Isn't that good news?"

"No. We need their sponsorship for at least another decade, maybe two. But they're getting impatient. The shareholders. Praxis was a very big, very expensive investment."

"Any portal is."

"Yes, but Praxis is an inhabitable world. A shirtsleeve world. That complicates things. Payday gets deferred until the scientists are satisfied."

"I slept with a scientist once," said Kai. "He wasn't satisfied. Neither was I. He wanted to keep trying."

I looked at him. "I did not need to know

that.".

Lopez interrupted quickly. "But this is the problem with any shirtsleeve world. The scientists are never satisfied. They keep postponing the profit-taking."

"Okay, I get it. The non-natives are getting restless. And if we vote for independence . . . then the Portal Authority has to negotiate trade agreements with whatever government we set up."

"We set up our own government and the Portal Authority loses control of the whole planet. On paper their loss would be measured in trillions."

"But they'd still be a trading partner. They could have a sustainable income for hundreds of years—"

"These shareholders aren't going to be here for hundreds of years. They want their payoff now.

"So they could sell their investments, I mean that's what they'd do on Luna."

"Yes, they could. But there's another option. Like I said, it's chatter. But it's very disturbing chatter. Enough to be worrisome."

Kai and I looked at each other. Lopez frowned, pursed his lips, shook his head. He didn't want to say it, as if speaking the possibility might make it real. He got up and went to the galley and poured himself a glass of orange juice. Kai reached over and squeezed my hand.

Lopez came back. He stood in the doorway, the glass still in his hand. "Some of them have been looking at the insurance policies. They've been asking what happens if the portal crashes? Would the investors be covered? Not that anyone would deliberately crash the portal, but what if, right?"

"That's not possible," Kai said. "There are safety measures in place."

Lopez nodded agreement. "Yes. There are. But they've never been tested."

I said, "So what would it take to crash a portal?"

"It would require a major disaster. We've studied the possibilities. Most of them are unlikely. But not all. That's why most of the stations are buried deep. That's why there are triple airlocks on both sides. We've run simulations."

"And . . . ?"

"It would require a thermonuclear event."

"So you don't allow—"

"No, we don't. But we don't have the manpower to inspect every pod. There are shippers we think we can trust—"

"And?"

"And there are always possibilities. There are more ways to destroy something than ways to protect it." He came in and sat down again. He put the empty glass to the side. "We're dealing with some very dangerous people. These are people who specialize in profiting from disasters. A fire wipes out a neighborhood? They go in and buy up the empty land. Do they start the fires? It's been suggested. Well, they don't start them, but somebody does. Don't take it personally, it's just business. You can build a very lucrative business out of other people's losses. Crashing the portal would be their biggest opportunity yet."

"I don't understand," said Kai "Where's the profit in that?"

"Insurance," Lopez replied.

I explained, "Most of the portals are insured through Lloyd's of Luna."

"Who are they?" Kai asked.

"It's a gigantic insurance cartel. They insure anything and everything—they can insure a pianist's hands, they can insure a herd of bison. They can insure an athlete's legs. They're gamblers. They take bets on probabilities. The thing about gambling, the house always wins. And Portal insurance is the best game in town, because the house has never had to pay."

"But if a portal crashed—? Could Lloyd's cover it?"

"Lloyd's isn't a single company. It's a cartel. A portal costs billions of plastic dollars. No single company can afford to insure the whole investment, the loss would be so big, it would put them out of business. So multiple companies each buy their own piece of the risk. If a portal ever crashes, each company only has to pay their own share, whatever they could afford. But the total loss is covered and nobody goes bankrupt. The members of the cartel even insure each other against critical losses. Everybody wins. The Portal Authority cashes the check and walks away from the investment with a wheelbarrow full of plastic dollars."

"But what about Praxis?"

"They don't care. They don't have to. They're the capital, not the labor. So you tell me. What happens to us if the portal crashes?"

He thought about it. "There's no way to go back. There's no communication, no supplies, no support. We're on our own. Isolated. Abandoned." He reached over and grabbed my hand.

I turned to Lopez, "Would we survive?"

"For a while, yes. Long term?" He shrugged. "Maybe. We need the portal. We're not sustainable yet. Not for a long time. But we have a lot of smart people here. We've got the libraries. We've got the fabbers. We could build the tools. It might be possible. It wouldn't be easy."

We sat in silence for a bit. Kai got up to make tea. This conversation had gone on longer than any of us had intended.

"So . . . if I understand this. Our independence is seen as a threat. If we follow through, they crash the portal?"

"Uh-huh."

"That seems a little extreme. What if maybe all this chatter you're hearing is deliberate. Maybe it's to scare us into accepting the continuing control of the Portal Authority."

"That's the obvious thought. It is something we'd considered. Yes, maybe it's just a ploy. But maybe it isn't. What is it you always say? Follow the money. Where's the biggest payday? Do you trust their better natures?"

"I don't even trust my better nature."

"I do," Lopez said. "Kai does."

"A year ago, I would have said, 'I don't have a dog in this fight.' Now, I do." I pointed to Kai, coming back with a tray.

"Well, yes. I have been called a son of a bitch," he said, setting down the tray. "But I'm not responsible for my mother's bad habits, only my own." He began pouring.

I looked across to Lopez. "So you think this is a real possibility?"

"I don't know. But we're already filing injunctions to transfer control of the portal to a holding company, on the grounds of deliberate mismanagement. It probably won't work, but the delays will buy us some time." To me, he said, "No, you're not the only lawyer on the payroll."

"Who else?"

"Kulik. Singer. Valada. Do you know them?"

"I know Valada. She can be dangerous."

"That's why we hired her." He took a deep

breath. "Anyway, that's the context. Now the content."

"There's more?"

He nodded. "Have some tea." He turned to Kai. "You might want to order up dinner. This is going to take a while."

THE FAST TRACK

And that's how Kai and I ended up on a fast train back to Earth—a high priority pod-train that could not be shuttled off to the side for other traffic. It would be three days of direct travel.

First, Coordinator Dolan's grand tour was a public relations success. The polls gave him a seven-point boost in favorables. The draft of the proposed constitution was greeted skeptically, but not antagonistically. Enough of it made sense that there was no serious critical opposition.

Second, Kai and I had somehow established ourselves as the love story of the year. We were part of the tour's success.

Third, I didn't embarrass myself. I nodded politely, listened to everything, and thanked everyone for their thoughts. Even Kai was impressed.

But that's not why we had to go back to

Earth.

If anyone had asked, and I'm sure that several people did, we had certain legal matters that needed our immediate attention.

I carried a declaration of Praxis Citizenship, which would supersede any Lunar-based contracts, including my own indenture, but also a letter of credit so I couldn't be sued for any debts related to the invalidated indenture.

Kai carried his own set of documents, declaring total independence from any Earth-based familial entanglements. He was legally disowning them.

And with Lopez's help, the two of us were scheduled to have Pope Juanita of the Church of the Chocolate Bunny sanctify our vows in the Lunar Cathedral—not really a cathedral as much as a lava tube with delusions of grandeur, and suitably decked out as a convention center, an amphitheater, a ballroom, a skating rink, a sports venue, or a church, depending on who made the reservation.

It wasn't the best cover story, but it was legitimate and the best we could do on short notice. It was also just surreal enough to be believable.

We traveled with diplomatic passports, a necessity for the fast-track pod-train, but we did not represent Praxis in any official capacity, our goals were personal. Yes, the black hats would be watching us, but nothing we intended would give them reason to be suspicious.

We took care of our legal business quickly. Praxis had agents on Earth who could file all the appropriate papers. All we had to do was sign the release forms. We gave them the manifests of everything that had been pre-ordered from Praxis and left them to supervise the packing and loading.

Then we did the tourist things. We went on a glittership tour, floating above the land. We saw the crumpled half of the statue on its little island and the brutal ruins at the south end of the city, and the Hall of Heroes in center of a carefully kept garden, and finally all the way up to Vermont to see the Autumn foliage.

Then we began to prepare for our return. We shopped. We did a lot of shopping. We had a long list of things that others had asked us to bring back, but we intended even more shopping than that.

And also maybe just a little bit of casual smuggling. Just enough to seem normal.

Except one of those items wouldn't be what it pretended to be. We'd pick it up on Earth and pretend it was a last minute impulse buy, some weird little game for the guys at Stonekettle, and toss it into the same bag with all the other gifts, some old-fashioned books, camera accessories, music libraries, Solar Expansion add-on sets, a lot of fancy chocolates, multiple packages of seeds, lots of coffee, some jars of French mustard, multiple jars of jams and jellies and pickles and sauces, especially salsa, and an insulated box of summer sausages and Darby Sage cheese that Lopez liked—also a large case of makeup kits, skirts and dresses, seductive tops, capes, wigs, feather boas, ballgowns, tiaras, necklaces, bracelets, jewelry of all kinds, a large variety of outrageous fabrics, and a few other inappropriate items for the boy-girls at Dorian.

Kai looked over the purchases and remarked that we were going to be very popular everywhere.

"What else should we pick up?"

"I think we overbought."

"Probably. But as long as there's room in the pod, we should keep buying. Right?"

Because the observable purpose of the trip was to bring back to Praxis all the things that were too difficult to import. That's why we had diplomatic passports. We weren't the first emissaries who pretended to have business on Earth just so they could come home with arms loaded.

There were always a few things that the Portal Authority did not want us importing. Like coffee beans. Something about import duties. That's why everything went into the diplomatic pouch, a very big diplomatic pouch, which they were forbidden by international law to inspect. They could scan the pouch, but they couldn't open it. As long as we weren't smuggling C5 or

C6, we were good to go.
        So we went.

INTERRUPTION

The pod-train went from Earth to Luna, where it picked up two more cars, then onto Mars. Two more cars. We stayed in our compartment and kept our pod locked. From Mars to Ceres, where we dropped off a car, then to Sedna and after that, the long slog through all the stations between here and there.

I crawled into bed with Kai and we held each other for a while and talked about nothing in particular. We kissed a little, but not much, we were both tired, physically as well as emotionally, but Kai said he couldn't sleep and got out of bed. He moved his pillows next to me and disappeared somewhere in the bathroom.

I had almost fallen asleep when they broke in.

I don't know how they got in. Maybe they had been aboard since before we left Earth. There were two of them and they were big and ugly. The big was by birth. The ugly was not. They had guns.

The light came on abruptly. I barely had time to sit up, gasping. But before I could say, "What the fu—?"

The first shot missed. I felt a sudden blast of heat all across my right side.

They never got a second shot.

Kai stepped out of the bathroom and blazed them both.

None of it happened like in the videos with lots of fighting and thrashing and broken furniture flying in all directions. They just looked surprised and collapsed. There wasn't any blood or noise or screaming, just a muffled *woof* and then a dark smoking scorch across their chests where the charges hit.

The whole thing was over so fast, I still wasn't sure what had happened. Or why.

Kai went over to them, kicked their guns to the far corners of the cabin, and shot them again. First in the chest, then in the head. He bent to each one, maybe looking to see if either was still breathing, maybe looking to see if he recognized them, or maybe just looking, but he didn't touch either.

He straightened and called for a pair of bots to come in and remove the bodies. I didn't recognize either of them. And I didn't see where they entered from. They looked industrial and they went to work immediately. I didn't watch.

I pointed at the bots. I pointed at the

bodies. I pointed at the door. I pointed at Kai. Some sounds came out of my throat. They weren't coherent.

Kai watched for a moment. He shook his head. He looked shaken. He said to the floor, "I did not want to do that. I really did not. No, I did not."

He sat down on the edge of the bed and put his head in his hands for a long moment and began one of his breathing exercises. Five counts to inhale. Five counts to hold. Five counts to exhale. Five counts before inhaling again. He did it five times. Or six. I lost count.

Finally he straightened and looked to me. "Are you all right."

For the first time, I noticed my entire right side felt burned. "Uh—" I gasped and turned so he could see—my longshirt was scorched. He pulled at it and it came away in pieces. My whole right side looked pink.

"Not too serious," he said.

"It really hurts."

"Sorry about that."

But I was looking at the bed. His side of it was charred and still smoking. "They were aiming at you!"

"Unh-unh. You were the target, but I'm the dangerous one."

I started shaking. "Kai—" I looked after the bots, just moving out. I couldn't speak.

He saw. He put a hand on my shoulder. I

gasped in pain.

"Sorry." He pulled back. "Let me get some salve."

He got up. "Are you going to be okay?"

"You saved my life. Both our lives! They were going to kill us."

He sat down again. "Would you like to scream for a while? Sometimes that helps."

"You've done this before?"

"Only in drills."

"Drills?"

"I'm your bodyguard, remember? I trained for this."

"This—?" I pointed at the empty floor.

"Not this specifically, but . . . yes."

"You killed them."

"Yes, I did."

I remembered something then, something he'd admitted. He didn't want to do this. He really didn't. "Kai?"

He hesitated.

"Are you going to be all right?"

"Eventually, yes. It might take a while." He shook me away. "Let me get some salve for your shoulder."

He got up again, disappeared into the bathroom, then came back quickly. He started applying it gingerly. "This might hurt for a minute, but it will dull the pain." It was cold, then hot, then cold again.

"How's that?"

"Better. Thank you."

He worked in silence, his hands sliding up and down my whole right side. I let him go on, long after the pain had ebbed. Finally, he asked, "Is it working?"

"Yes, but don't stop."

He stopped anyway. "I'm sorry," he said. "I'm not going to be very easy to live with for a while."

I skipped the obvious joke. "Just tell me that you'll be all right."

"Well, I'll be a lot better than those guys."

A thought occurred to me. A very unpleasant thought. I didn't speak it.

"Hold me?" he asked.

"C'mere."

We held onto each other for a couple years, then he let go. He looked at the ceiling, the walls, the floor, as if looking for an escape, there was none, finally he turned back to me and admitted, "This is why I made sure wherever we went, we were always in the middle of a crowd, or someplace where an attack would be inconvenient."

"You knew?"

"Yeah."

"And you didn't tell me?"

"I didn't want to worry you. And I didn't want you looking over your shoulder every few minutes, noticing how they were following us."

"They were following us?"

"They were waiting for us from the moment we arrived on Earth. But they couldn't get to us there. And it would have been inconvenient to try anything on Mars or even Sedna, any place with a real police force. Out here, far way from everything, this was better."

"But how did they—?"

"They were in that last cargo container. The one that supposedly held extra supplies. If they had succeeded, this pod would have disappeared enroute. Probably at North Station. That's a bad place. You have to pay a fat transmission fee to guarantee that your pod gets through. Once we were dead, those guys would probably sell the cargo, a little extra bonus for them, and North Station would sell the pod to a mining company to use as an extra dorm."

"I'm not very good at humility—"

"I know."

"—shut up and let me finish. I'm trying to compliment you. Apparently I have lived a very sheltered life. There is so much here that I've never had to deal with, all this stuff that I don't know—"

"When are you going to get to the compliment part—?"

I put two fingers across his lips. "I am sorry that I underestimated you. You're good. You really are."

"Yes, I am. Better than you know." He faced me, with an intense expression. "You'd have been dead without me."

"Twice over. At least."

"Because I'm careful," Kai said. "And I don't want Lopez yelling at me. And I'm too young to be a widow."

"Widower."

"Whatever."

I grabbed him and held him. He held me just as tight.

Abruptly, I pulled back. "Are we safe now? Are there others? Will they try again?"

"No. But—just to be sure, I'll tell the bots to inspect every cargo container for signs of life. We can monitor from here." He looked around. "We'll have to repair the bed—"

"I am not going to sleep tonight. Maybe not until we get home."

Kai hesitated, then decided to say it anyway. "I'm not going to tell you they won't try again. But I don't think they'll try here."

"You're sure?"

"Of course not."

DISCOVERY

Just before the final leg of the trip, we were delayed at North Station. Some kind of official mix up, everybody was arguing with everybody.

Finally, Kai disembarked and met with the Station Monitor. The man looked annoyed at the interruption. Kai said something to him, the man's expression shifted abruptly and he waved Kai back on board. A few moments later, we rolled through the portal.

I asked Kai, "What was that about?"

"He said that the manifest for our pod wasn't in order and he needed to inspect the entire train. I explained to him that this was a high-priority transit and we had been cleared straight through from Earth. He said he was supposed to meet Bert and Ernie. Code names probably. I told him that they were in no condition to meet with him. He didn't like that. I invited him to see for himself. Would he like to join them? I could arrange that. I was very polite. I also pointed out that traffic was backing up, but if he insisted—apparently, that was enough. He said we should go."

Half a day later, we were finally back on Praxis.

I still wasn't ready to relax.

Despite Kai's steady reassurances, I saw shadows everywhere. I asked him how he was able to stay so calm. He said, "I'm not calm. I'm just pretending."

Lopez and his assistants, Karl, Sebastian, and Glenn, arrived to manage the unloading. Glenn was the large one. The hatch to the cargo level slid open, Lopez looked at the wall of containers and took a step back. Without taking his eyes away from the fully packed hold, he asked, "How much did you guys spend?"

I told him.

To his credit, he didn't blink.

"And you didn't have any trouble with customs?"

"I'm from Luna. This is something I know how to do. They asked for a list of everything we bought. I told them it was all in the diplomatic pouch. They insisted. I refused. They got uglier. They were already ugly. I didn't think they could get uglier. But maybe that's a necessary skill for petty bureaucrats."

"And . . . ?"

"I gave in. I gave them the receipts, all of

them. I told them we didn't have a digital file yet, we were still cataloging everything. It was a very thick stack of paper." I pantomimed half a meter. "That kinda slowed them down. I think they riffled through all those receipts, just to look like they were doing something, or maybe to reassure themselves it was all receipts and not anything dangerous, like a book, but finally they just said, 'This isn't acceptable. You'll have to buy a waiver.' Really? Is that what they call it now. But Kai handed them a very thick envelope, and they slapped a sticker on the pod and told us to go away. All those receipts, all that paper—just props. It's always about the envelope."

Lopez nodded. "Nicely done."

"We got off lucky. We were expecting worse."

"It could have been worse, but the other side had their attention elsewhere. While you were gone, we held our first military preparedness games."

Lopez almost looked happy. "It was a good show. You would have enjoyed it. We invited representatives of the Portal Authority to review. Well, not before we had an argument about it in the committee, a very long and very loud argument, but eventually we all got tired of arguing and it would have been impolite to not invite them, so we did. Unfortunately, we held the event on the far side of Pelz, a little too far for any of their representatives to travel, so they politely declined to attend in person. But they did send drones. Several hundred of them. They had eyes everywhere. I guess they wanted us to know that nothing we did would go unobserved. So we showed them."

Lopez allowed himself a hint of a grin. "Unfortunately, the exercise did not go well. Our troops were clumsy, they ended up firing on each other, and both sides tried to surrender to each other. The Society For Creative Anarchy would have been more convincing as a threat. Apparently, Praxis is not yet ready for a real rebellion."

"I guess not," I said.

Very casually, Lopez leaned sideways to me and lowered his voice. "I heard you had a little incident."

"It wasn't little."

He looked from me to Kai and back again. "Are you okay?"

"No." I said. I looked to Kai. "I don't think he is either. He's pretending he's fine, but—"

Kai held up his hands, a gesture of denial. "Let's not talk about it here."

"Right," said Lopez. "It was a long exhausting trip. Say no more. Maybe when you're ready. Meanwhile—"

He stepped past us and looked deep into the cargo level of the pod. Multiple containers completely filled the space. "All right. Move 'em out," he said. We had to wait while the cargo bots rolled them out, one after the other. Lopez looked to me. "Which one?"

"That one, I think." I pointed.

"You think?"

"You wanted it to be confusing." I handed him a flat black card, the key. Lopez pressed it to the seal. The container unlocked and opened. He stared at the stacks of boxes inside, not sure if he should laugh or frown.

I said, "I wanted to make it as hard as possible for anyone to get into our cargo. Especially as we were locked into a three o'clock departure."

He grunted something that sounded like approval. He was already sorting through the boxes. Karl and Sebastian and Glenn, the human giant, stepped in to help him. They unloaded half the boxes from the container before they found the one he wanted.

"Ahh," he said. It took all three of them to grapple the thing, an industrial, man-sized box secured in a heavy plastic frame. It had multiple handles and sat on a rolling platform. They moved it slowly, carefully. Lopez walked around it, studying it intensely. I followed him. The security panels all glowed green. Finally, Lopez looked to me, then to Kai. "You have no idea what this is, do you?"

We shook our heads.

"This—if it works, if it's everything we hope it is—makes it impossible for the Portal

Authority to shut us down. They might be able to detect it, maybe not—I don't know. But this gives us leverage."

"What is it?"

"The last curse out of Pandora's box. Hope."

SMUGGLING

I'd only seen a containment like that once before, and then only from a distance, but I did not speak my suspicions aloud. Not here. Not yet.

I had two good reasons to be paranoid. I did not want a third. What if the black hats finally sent someone competent?

But I didn't have time to think about it. Lopez said, "You and Kai are coming with me now." He pointed. "Go stand over there. You have luggage? We'll get it. I'm taking you to the farm, you should be safe there. No more chances."

Things were happening all around us. Lopez's assistants slid the mysterious containment into a large crate labeled topsoil. It smelled of manure. Very clever. They pushed the crate against the wall, one more in a long line of identical crates, all bad smelling.

He opened his phone. "Dolan," he said. He waited to connect. I couldn't hear the other side of the conversation. I assumed, Dolan said something like, "Hello," or "What now?" Lopez said calmly, "The boys are back. All good. And they brought you that stupid French mustard you like. I'll send it across tonight. You're welcome. Later." He folded up the phone and slid it back into his pocket. He had said a lot more than any casual listener would suspect.

As a rule, we now had to suspect that the enemy—yes, we had to think of them as the enemy now, an attempt on one's life does crystallize one's thinking—we had to assume that the enemy had eyes and ears everywhere. Especially here.

This dock was triple-shielded and there were interference generators hanging from the ceiling. But the bad guys could have planted sleepers anywhere in the pod or the cargo, awakening only later when it was possible to narrowcast what they'd seen and heard here. That was probably why customs had waived a more thorough inspection.

We followed Lopez and the line of topsoil crates through the tunnels to another loading dock. This one led to . . . an airship?

"I thought Praxis couldn't afford any vacuum bubbles."

"We can't. This doesn't exist."

"Um—"

"Need to know," Lopez said.

Of course.

I thought about it anyway.

There was a lot of cargo going back and forth between all the outlying stations, a lot of smuggling too. I wondered what Praxis was trading. Probably fresh fruit. Sure, load up the kitchens on the outbound trains, it's all considered perishable. If it doesn't come back . . . okay.

I was probably wrong, but I could see how that might work.

The crates went into the cargo deck. We went up a ramp to the passenger level. The hatch sealed behind us.

"Watch," said Lopez. He pointed toward a display.

External monitors revealed our progress. The ship lifted off its cradle, only a couple of meters and moved slowly forward, into the next chamber, where it was blasted with water, foam, disinfectants, more water, more foam, another round of disinfectants, more water—

"We don't want to introduce any of Earth's biology into Praxis. It works both ways. This will take a while." He pointed. "Let's go downstairs. I want to show you something."

"Downstairs" meant the cargo hold, where Karl, Sebastian, and Glenn waited patiently. This close, he seemed a lot bigger. One of the crates stood apart from the others. It had already been pulled open and the mysterious containment had been removed.

"We ready?" Lopez asked.

Big Glenn nodded.

"Let's roll."

Big Glenn pulled up a hatch in the floor. A ladder led down a dark shaft. Karl and Sebastian climbed down the ladder. Big Glenn rolled the containment over, looped a rope through its handles, lifted it without apparent strain, and began lowering it down the shaft.

From below, Karl called, "We got it. Securing it now."

Big Glenn pointed at the hole. "Next?"

Lopez gestured to me and Kai. "Go on, I'll follow."

Kai went first. I climbed down after him into a very cramped space, some kind of vehicle. A moment later Lopez dropped down, then Big Glenn. He secured the hatch above us. "And we're green."

Sebastian and Karl were sitting up front at the controls. The containment had been shoved in the back. Kai and I parked ourselves on a side bench, facing Big Glenn and Lopez on the opposite side. Lopez opened his phone and studied the screen. "Okay. The airship is clear."

Karl did something at the board over his head, Sebastian grabbed his handles and we moved, suddenly turning to the right. "The airship is a decoy," Lopez said across to us. "Sorry there're no windows. We're inside the storage bay of a regularly scheduled maintenance bot."

We felt the separate footsteps of the machine as it padded through the tunnel, but the ride was smooth. Once outside, its gait changed as the vehicle tilted across uneven ground. "The airship is going to Pelz. We're going the opposite way."

"You think they'll attack the airship?"

"No, but just in case, no one's aboard, not even the pilots. They're driving by remote. Not the first time. Praxis can throw some serious weather at us. We'd rather lose a ship than a pilot."

I frowned, thinking. "We're headed toward the ocean?"

"The unfinished harbor," Lopez said. "We'll be underground in less than an hour."

INSIDE

The underground offices and warehouses had been dug in first, more than a decade ago, but they remained unfurnished. Three of the docks had been completed, but none of the cranes had been installed. The uncertain behavior of the seas during dark winter and brighter summer had forced a pause in construction pending further long-term study. So far, the simulations had all proven accurate, but most shirtsleevers were less sanguine. They said it bluntly. "Praxis is a bitch."

Less colloquially, Praxis didn't much care for human things. She had her own ideas how she wanted to conduct herself and alien creatures popping in from another dimension were not part of her plan. Nevertheless, here we were.

Sebastian drove the vehicle away from the existing roadbed. One day there would be tracks leading toward the harbor, but that had been postponed until the future of the harbor was decided. We wound our way back and forth and up over a long, rugged slope that would have directed us inland if we'd followed it, but there was a narrow cut between two of the upthrust layers of sedimentary rock and he ducked sideways through it. For just those few moments, we were all holding onto the tie-down handles and clamps to keep from sliding into each other.

We came out on a steep cliff overlooking the ocean and Sebastian turned right and headed for Real-Soon-Now Harbor. He had to pick his way carefully, there was a lot of loose rock and gravel here. He didn't want to start an avalanche. But eventually, we padded up to a hatch that looked like it had not slid open for years. He looked back to us, grinning. "The Beagle has landed."

"I am not—oh, never mind." I folded my arms. Beside me, Kai leaned his head on my shoulder.

Lopez opened a channel and said, "Speak friend and enter." The hatch rolled aside as if it had been oiled this morning. Sebastian drove us inside and the hatch slid shut behind us. The vehicle padded down a dark unlit tunnel, its spotlights the only illumination.

Eventually, we reached a large industrial chamber that looked like it was waiting for the rest of the machinery to be installed. It seemed vaguely familiar. "Looks like a transit station,"

Kai remarked.

"Yes, it could be. Maybe someday, it will be," Lopez said. "Just not right now."

Sebastian brought the vehicle to a stop, Karl fiddled with his overhead controls, and the machine sank down on its legs so we could climb out. We were met by a squad of four men in jumpsuits. They looked excited and eager and determined to get to work.

Lopez made hasty introductions. "Code names only, from here on." He pointed toward an older man. "This is Rottweiler. He'll be running the installation team. Over here, Collie, Retriever, and Poodle."

"Do I need a code name?"

"Nah. But they do. In case you get captured and tortured."

"You're joking, right?"

"Do I look like I'm joking?"

"No."

"That's why you're here. You and Kai. For your own protection. No more little incidents."

"It wasn't little."

"You survived, didn't you?"

"Excuse me—?" That was Rottweiler. "Can we get started?"

Lopez pointed around. "As soon as we sweep the facility."

"My team just finished a sweep—"

"And Bean and Carrot—" He indicated Karl and Sebastian. "—will confirm. In case you hadn't heard, there was an attack on the delivery team, so we're triple-checking everything."

"Was anyone hurt?"

"Only the attackers. I assume they were more surprised than hurt. We couldn't do an autopsy." Lopez nodded to Bean and Carrot, they began unloading cases of scanning equipment. "If our sweep comes up green, we'll unload the package."

Rottweiler didn't look happy, but he didn't argue.

Bean and Carrot took a long time examining every nook and cranny, they doubled back and reinspected them, possibly looking for more nooks or crannies. But eventually, the scan came up green.

Lopez nodded to Rottweiler. "The package is yours."

"Thank you." He turned and directed his team to board the transport and unload the containment.

"This is going to take a while," said Lopez. "Let's get some lunch. Or breakfast. Or dinner? What time do you have?" He pointed us toward what would have been the offices, if this station were operative. "There's a galley behind the living quarters. Don't worry, we're not poaching. We brought enough supplies to sustain us for a few months. I hope we won't need to be here that long."

"Huh?"

"Oh, I'm sorry. I forgot to tell you. The pod you came in on. It went missing. Nobody knows what happened to it. Or to you. Close your mouth. It's for your own protection. You have to disappear for a while. You and Kai are fugitives, suspected of murder. Unofficially, of course. Because they don't want to admit they sent the assassins, but—upstairs knows that something is up. Upstairs isn't happy. And when upstairs isn't happy, everyone else is miserable. Well, it's their own damn fault, but—yeah, you're here now."

"For how long?"

"Well . . ." Lopez scratched his ear thoughtfully. "If I remember correctly, you still have two and a half years on your contract, so . . ."

"So?"

"So . . ." He clapped me on the shoulder. "Let's get lunch."

LUNCH

Lunch was sandwiches and coffee. Not the best meal we'd ever had on Praxis, but maybe the most relaxing. We sat. We ate. We looked at each other and said nothing. We were tired. We'd all been through a lot. But for the moment, we were done. There was nothing else to do. It was all up to Rottweiler and his team, Collie, Retriever, and Poodle.

I looked over to Kai. He was tired and withdrawn. I didn't know what to say to him, so I just reached over and patted his knee. Lopez nodded acknowledgment.

And then his phone beeped.

He opened it and listened for a moment.

His expression tightened.

"Thanks for telling me," he said and closed his phone.

"They know something's up. The corporation just ordered Dolan to stop distributing a draft constitution and dissolve the government. They're calling it an unlawful assembly, therefore it violates the charter."

"What if he doesn't—?"

"They didn't say."

"Did they give him a deadline?"

"Immediately."

"What's he going to do?"

Lopez took a breath. "He told them he wanted it in writing. But before they sent over the paperwork, they should try folding it into a ball with lots of sharp corners and see if they can stuff it where the sun don't shine."

"How did they take it?" Kai asked.

"They hung up."

"So we're at war?"

"I don't think you could call it that. A war is a conflict of countries. In their eyes, we're an unauthorized labor movement. I dunno, maybe we're an insurrection. They have called us a colony in some of their public statements, so maybe we're a rebellion. I'm not clear on the legal terms." Lopez looked to me. "Arbiter?"

"Above my pay grade, I'm afraid. I think the definition depends on which side wins and writes the history books. But all of those things you listed usually involve violence. What can we expect?"

"Not much, not really. They don't have ships in the harbor. They don't have ships in orbit. They don't have an army massed on our border. They have no place from which to launch missiles. So conventional war isn't practical. If they intend any kind of military action, they'd have to ship men and materiel all the way up the line. Not impossible, but we'd know about that kind of traffic long before they reached North Station. You really can't stage an invasion from North Station. It just isn't workable."

He was still thinking aloud. "And then there's the problem of the portal. If we knew they were sending troops—and we would—then we could simply close our side of the portal. They'd have to blast through the airlocks. They could, but it would violate the portal agreements, and that's a set of conventions they helped write. If they were to violate the portal agreements, they'd be subject to sanctions by all the other signers. They'd lose their place at the table. Their part of the Portal Authority would be forfeit. The other corporations would love to take over some of their properties."

"So they really don't have any options, do they?"

"No, they have one. Crash the portal. Destroy the station, call it a tragic disaster, and cash the insurance check. Oh, there'd be investigations of all kinds, but without any access to this side, there'd be no evidence. It wouldn't be that hard. They could put a bomb on a cargo train. That would do it. Yes, we could shut down any suspicious traffic, we could shut down all traffic, but Praxis is a long way from self-sufficiency. If we comply, they win. If we don't comply, they can still win."

I leaned back in my chair and folded my arms. Lopez looked across at me. "What?"

"You, Dolan, the whole committee, all of you—you're not stupid."

He waited for me to say the rest.

"You've been planning for this from the beginning. This is your endgame."

"Yes? What's your point?"

"Nobody pokes a bear by accident. What are you not telling us?"

Lopez looked at the time. He stood up. "Right. Come with me."

CONTEXT

We followed Lopez back into the unfinished station. From there he led us through a long series of tunnels to another set of chambers.

"Wait, those are airlocks, aren't they."

"They will be as soon as we activate them. Probably tonight. Follow me."

We came out on a platform looking down at a set of tracks leading to—

"Huh? That's a portal—!"

"Yes, it is. Or it will be soon. We still have to install it and test it and then activate the connection and expand the portal to a functional size. This place was originally built to be a portal station so the line could be extended outward. But the corporation was overbought. They couldn't afford the investment. And they didn't want to risk a blowout, like Montana. They could have lost their entire investment in Praxis. So they shut it down. This was all decades ago."

"But it's still—"

"Shut up and let me explain."

I shut.

"We didn't have a portal. Not then. And we didn't have the technology to attempt one. But we'd invested a lot in the construction, so we—well, the committee at the time, thought we might be able to convert it into a shipping port, not a bad idea, but that got put on hold too. Again, too big an investment for impatient shareholders. They didn't see the point. But here on Praxis, we started using it as a seasonal shelter. Bright summer. Dark winter. A lot of shirtsleevers come here to wait out the seasons. There's more than enough room."

"Okay, I got all that"

"It's what we call 'necessary exposition,'" said Lopez. "Setting context. So you'll understand the content."

"I'm a lawyer," I said.

"Don't apologize. That's why we hired you. You were part of the distraction."

"So you never wanted a constitution at all —"

"Actually, you convinced us that we needed one. That's the trouble with lawyers. You're good at making yourself essential."

"That's because human beings can't get along with each other without laws. Agreements. And then after you make your agreements, you look for ways to ignore them.

That's why lawyers are essential. We argue for you. The good ones can argue either side, depending on who has the most money."

"Yes, thank you. We had that conversation before I went to Luna."

"So you bought a portal," I said. "And you smuggled it in. I don't see what good that does you."

"How much do you understand how portals work."

"They're a hole in space. That's as far as I got."

"That's as far as most people get. Okay, more context." He pointed to a bench. "You want to sit?"

Kai and I sat. He reached over and grabbed my hand.

Lopez went to a nearby worktable. He pawed through a scattering of tools and wires and tubes that somebody hadn't yet discarded. He came back with a pair of plastic rings. He put them back-to-back. "Okay, imagine these rings are a portal that I've just created." He pushed his hand through the hole. "When the two halves of it are joined together like this, the portal is useless. But—" He separated the rings, holding them apart, one in each hand. "If you could put one over here and the other over here, then you can step into one and step out the other without going through the intervening space. Everybody understands that much. We imagine that there's some kind of subspace tunnel from one to the other. Maybe there is, maybe there isn't. I'll leave that to the experts—"

"I thought you were a Portal Master—"

"I'm a Portal Master, not a Quantum Mechanic. Now stop interrupting—" He waved one of the rings at us. "It was demonstrated by the Montana blowout that if you destroy one side of the portal, the other side destructs as well. And a lot of the surrounding countryside too. But —and this is where it gets interesting. There's a theory, nobody's tested it yet, but the math is solid—that if you could put one side of a portal on a portal train and pass it up the line, then you wouldn't just have a subspace tunnel connecting two rings, you'd have another subspace tunnel running through them and that would make it impossible to shut down the holding rings."

He looked at us. "That's not clear, is it? Wait. Here, you hold this ring, you hold that one. This is the way it was explained to me. He went back to the table and grabbed a spool of wire. He threaded the wire through the rings that Kai and I were holding. "Now, imagine that wire is the connection between two portal rings. Supposedly that interior connection makes it impossible to break the external connection. It sounds good, but it hasn't been tested. The better part of theory says that if we could shut down the portal rings, the ones that you two are holding, even if that connection disappeared, the portal connection that the wire represents would still be present. That's theory. We haven't tested that either. But neither has the corporation. You have questions?"

"So you had us smuggle one side of a portal from Earth to here. All the way through the entire branch. And you're going to power it up to full size, right?"

"Uh-huh?"

"And Praxis will have its own portal, one that we control here."

"Yep."

"Where's the other side of it? If I stepped through, where would I be?"

"North Dakota."

CONTENT

"**W**ait. What?"

Lopez sighed. "It's bad enough I have to teach you Praxis history, I have to teach you Earth history too? What is it with people from Earth, a commitment to ignorance?"

"I'm from Luna."

"Same difference. Earth's back yard."

"Please—?"

"Yes, all right. The Montana Station failed because someone was stupid or impatient or wasn't following established safety protocols. We can argue about that all week. But Montana was an experiment. What if you don't open the portal to its other side? What if you open it to a random address, some place where you expect to find another world? We do that all the time now. We just don't do it on Earth. Because you don't want to accidentally open a portal to the inside of a star. Still with me? Here's where it gets good. Montana was not the only station. Three more were under construction. Two in South Dakota. One in North Dakota. Tracks were being laid to connect all of them. When Montana blew out, construction was halted on all three and no further Earth-based portals were installed."

"Yes, I know that. Everybody does."

"Uh-huh. That's what everybody believes. Here's the fun part. A local portal was opened and even activated in the North Dakota station, but after the blowout it would have been politically dangerous to even admit it existed. So the other side of that portal was never shipped out. Shortly after the blowout, and probably because of it, the United States broke apart. The Northern Plains district took control of the stations. At first they didn't know what they had. The district was mostly an arm of the agricultural and mining interests in the states, but when they realized the possibilities, they very quietly decided to maintain those three stations against some time in the future they could reactivate them. Maybe eventually, there would be a safe way to open new portals. But then, subsequent administrations got preoccupied with crop failures and the competition from off-world mining companies and they had more immediate problems to solve. The whole thing is a long, complicated story with a lot of moving parts."

Lopez paused to look down at the

installation and the men working busily around it. "So now, look down. Do you know what that is? That's the other side of the North Dakota portal."

I faced him. "Okay. I'm impressed. Tell me how you got it."

"You brought it here, you and Kai, there was no other way. But to get the Dakotans onboard, that was a whole other challenge. We negotiated in secret for eighteen months. The result was a very secret treaty. If they'll support the independence of Praxis, then Praxis will give them an exclusive license to manage traffic through this portal. A win-win for both sides. We get sustainability, users get direct access and North Dakota becomes a major transport hub. Users get a shorter trip and won't have to pay toll charges for passing pods through every station between here and there. Well, just our transfer fee, but one tax is preferable to twenty. And North Dakota Transport becomes our trading partner, not our owner. We get independence and sustainability, they get a recharged economy. And the Portal Authority gets a pie in the face. What is it you always say? Follow the money."

He stopped and looked at us. "You want some more coffee?"

BLOWOUT

We went back to the kitchen to wait while the coffee brewed.

"How much does the Portal Authority know?"

"They know there's a portal. They don't know if it's here yet."

Kai spoke up. "They know. They know everything."

We both turned to look at him.

"It's my fault. I'm sorry. I don't expect you to forgive me. Either of you, but mostly you, Dar." He tugged the ring off his finger and pushed it into my hand

I pushed it back at him. He refused to take it. He pushed me away. "You're going to hate me."

"I can't imagine that."

"I can," Lopez said.

I stepped back from both of them. "What? Would one of you tell me what's going on here?"

Kai wouldn't look at me. He folded his

arms across his chest and stared at the floor. "I'm so stupid."

Lopez cleared his throat. "Kai has been spying on you."

"I knew that. He's been reporting to you since . . . forever."

"No," said Lopez. "He's also been reporting to the Portal Authority. They promised him privileges. Hard to resist those kinds of promises when all you've known is poverty and rejection. It looked like an escape route. The problem with that is that once someone outlives their usefulness, they become an annoying burden. It's cheaper to . . . yeah, your little incident."

I started to cross to Kai. His posture was rigid. He didn't want anyone near him. I stopped midstep. "Is that true?"

"I'm sorry, Dar. I told them everything."

I looked to Lopez. "And you knew?"

"There wasn't anything he could tell them that was critical. I said, more than once, you were only intended as a distraction. The real work . . ." He pointed toward the chamber containing the portal. " . . . was that."

"They tried to kill us," said Kai. "I'm an idiot. I thought they could be trusted—"

Lopez crossed to him. "You did the job you were supposed to do. Listen to me. We knew you were reporting to them from the very beginning. We could have let you go shirtsleeve, but they would have just planted someone else.

It was easier to use you as a channel for misinformation. Putting you with the Arbiter— I'm sorry, nobody expected the two of you to get married, let alone fall in love."

"You used me. They used me. Everybody used me. I'm just the tissue you throw away after."

"Yes, everyone used you," said Lopez. "Except your husband."

Kai didn't answer. He sniffled. He wiped his nose on his sleeve. "And I used him. I'm worse than all of you. He trusted me."

"Yeah, so what?" said Lopez. "That's how most relationships work. You use each other. The good relationships are where you enjoy it."

"Yeah, what do you know about it?"

Lopez took a breath. I knew that expression. I'd seen it enough times in court. "What do I know about it? I'll take you to the cemetery and show you what I know about it. Will that be good enough for you?" He crossed to Kai and grabbed him by the shoulders. "There's something you're missing, you little idiot. You saved his life. Does that mean anything to you? You saved his life and he held you close. He was there for you when you needed someone to just hold onto. So, yes—you used him. But he used you to practice a little empathy and caring, a couple of things he is notoriously not good at." He turned to me. "Am I right, Dar?"

I didn't answer.

Lopez let go of Kai. "Listen to me. Yes, you're an idiot. But you're his idiot—and he can be a jerk, but he's your jerk. And what the two of you have is something that a lot of people don't have. And both of you would be idiotic jerks to throw it all away now."

"We don't have anything anymore. I ruined it all."

I crossed to him then. I grabbed his hand and pushed the ring back onto his finger. "No. You didn't ruin anything. We have honesty now. That has to count for something."

Kai looked at his hand, at his finger, at the ring, and finally at me. His eyes were wet.

"I'm not quitting," I said to him. "I will not be one more person who throws you away. I am not giving you up."

Kai gulped. And then he threw himself into my arms and held on tight.

DECLARATIONS

"**A**bout fucking time," said Lopez.

"No," I said. "Fucking time will be after we rechannel."

"Wait. What? You haven't—"

Kai sniffled. "We've been having too much fun flirting."

"It's called foreplay," I said to Kai.

"There you go again, being pedantic."

"You married me."

"And I will again. As soon as you ask."

"I'm asking you now."

"Okay, yes."

"If you two are through—we have a revolution to attend to." He looked to Kai. "When was your last report to them?"

"Sedna. After they tried to, you know—I cut them off."

"Okay, good."

"But I'm still chipped. They can monitor my location."

"No, they can't." He pointed to Kai's ring. There's an interrupter in that. We turned it on when your train rolled through the last airlock. All they know is that you, or your body, got to Praxis. If our security measures worked, they might even think you and Dar are dead and their assassins have gone dark. But we'll have your chip fried. Or removed. As soon as it's convenient. No more spy games."

"You were our handler, right?"

He nodded. "I will admit, you two have been a lot to handle. But your part is over. All I need to do now is keep you safely hidden. The Portal Authority is about to get nasty."

We followed him back to the catwalk overlooking the Portal Chamber. "They've been training for this for months. It looks like they've finished testing the monitors and the fail-safes, I wish we had more time, but we don't. As soon as they lower it into position between the airlocks and seal the chambers and test for triple integrity—they can activate the connection." He looked at his phone. "So far, everything looks green. As soon as it's live, Dolan will broadcast our Declaration of Independence."

Lopez pocketed his phone and turned to me. "What's the polite way to tell your boss he's fired?"

"There is no polite way."

"The legal way . . . ?"

"There is no legal way. A declaration of

independence is a declaration of war." I added, Think of it from their side. You're stealing their property and claiming it as yours."

"They're not here. We are."

"They see you as highly paid employees."

"Then they should never have called us colonists."

"You hired an arbiter. Do you want an official response?"

"Is there a way to stop you?"

"No." I explained, "In the battle between labor and capital, it is usually capital that fails to understand that it is not a battle, but a partnership. Fail to service the partnership and the declaration of war is inevitable. That's a lesson that goes all the way back to . . . I dunno, maybe when the Praetorian Guard terminated Caligula? No, probably before that. But you get the point. Capital is greedy. It's built into the system."

"You're anti-capital?"

"No. I'm anti-stupid. Capital doesn't care about people. That's why it needs to be regulated before it becomes cancerous. That's why the constitution I gave to Coordinator Dolan is so dangerous. Not to us. To them."

"Yes. You have been an excellent distraction. My compliments."

His phone beeped. Lopez pulled it out of his pocket and stared at it. "The portal is live. Dolan has broadcast the declaration. And we are at war." He added, "Actually, we've been at war for a while, but now it's official."

ABOUT TIME

I awoke still curled up around Kai. He turned around to hug me. "I don't deserve you," he said.

"No, you don't. But you got me anyway."

He held me tight for a while.

"I don't want to lose you," he said.

"You can't," I said. "We're married."

"I am so sorry. I was so afraid . . ."

"Shh. I just wish you had told me sooner. I would have pretended to be even dumber."

"No. You were dumb enough."

"High praise indeed. Thank you." I pulled back enough to look into his eyes. "Is there anything else you need to tell me?"

"Well . . ." he hesitated.

"What?"

"I'm—"

"What?!"

"—not straight. I lied about that too. It wasn't a girl they caught me with. It was a boy."

"I did wonder," I admitted.

"You did?"

"It was the way you kissed. A little too enthusiastic."

"You kissed me back."

"Well, it would have been rude not to."

"So . . . if I said I wanted to consummate our marriage . . . ?"

"I think it would be appropriate."

"Even without rechanneling?"

"The way you kiss, I'm not sure I need it now."

"No, really. I mean it."

"You'll probably have to teach me the ins and outs—"

"I will even teach you the ups and downs."

He rolled back into my arms.

The parts that needed to be hard were hard. The parts that were supposed to be fun were even better.

WAR

Eventually, we put on some clothes and wandered back out to the galley. Lopez was just making coffee. He looked at us appraisingly. "I won't ask," he said.

"Good. 'Cause we're not telling."

"You don't have to. I can see it on your faces. Congratulations. Finally. You want coffee?"

"We'd love some. How goes the war?"

"As expected. They rejected our declaration as an act of terrorism. They don't even consider us a rebellion. So their response is a police action."

"And . . . ?"

"They tried to arrest the Coordinator."

"I assume that did not go well."

"No, it did not. The survivors have been detained. When we finally get around to appointing an arbiter, their cases will be fairly heard. Are you available?"

"I don't do death penalty cases," I said.

"Not ever?"

"I admit, there are exceptional situations. I'd have to study the precedents. Too many of them are iffy. But even where it might be justifiable, and I can think of three reasons, there's a lot of law to consider. The death penalty represents a difficult collision of justice and pragmatism, not to mention the moral aspects. But, if it's an issue, I strongly believe in self-defense—and I won't pretend that my feelings haven't been affected by recent personal experiences, but—if we consider that an assault on the community requires self-defense on the part of the community—" Hmm. "Let me think about it. If the law isn't just, then Barkis was right, the law is an ass."

"Who's Barkis?"

"How the Dickens should I know?"

"You're being literate again, aren't you?"

"It's a virtue, but I can live with it."

He handed me coffee and another mug to Kai, who had been watching the whole exchange with unconcealed amusement.

"Let's talk serious," Lopez said. He pointed toward the table.

We sat.

"They've seized the North Dakota station."

"But you expected that, right?"

He nodded. "The portal is live. So it's valuable. A direct portal between Praxis and Earth? Yes, very valuable. The Portal Authority is claiming ownership because the portal was stolen by one of their employees and installed by other of their employees."

"Except I was never employed by the Portal Authority."

"And neither were the techs who installed the portal and activated it. They were independent contractors brought in by independent operators. How would you rule, Arbiter?"

"I would have to recuse myself. Conflict of interest." I pointed to Kai. "A lot of interest."

"Please, spare me the details."

"You recruited me, you recruited him, what did you think would happen—?"

"All right, fine," he interrupted. He waved his hand around, as if indicating the entire situation. "You don't seem to be worried about any of this."

"No, I am not. Two reasons. First, we might be war criminals, but this is Argentina. Second, I am certain you have a plan. If you're not worried, I'm not."

"I'm worried," he said.

"Not enough."

"They're gathering an invasion force. They're going to send troops through the portal." He pointed in the direction of the installation. "That one."

"And . . . ?"

"And they'll die." He looked at me sharply.

"What?"

"On Luna, we had an unwritten rule. 'Nobody dies.' That goes all the way back to the first established stations. Later, it got modified, 'If we can prevent it, if we can save them, if we can do anything at all, nobody dies.' I was raised in that context. When I became an arbiter, it was the basis for all decisions. Justice does not demand death. Humans do."

"Go on."

"Those troops, those young men—I don't care what they believe, how deeply they've been indoctrinated, how much they believe in their cause, or even how much they regard us as the enemy. They're just following the orders of people who regard their lives as expendable. Yes, we have to defend ourselves. It's what I said about self-defense. But . . ." I took a breath. Listen to me. "Violence has to be the last course of action, not the first. Only the incompetent or the cowardly or the very stupid start with violence. Those men might have families. They might have lovers. Or they might be assholes without empathy. I don't care. Just tell me this. Is there no other course of action?"

Lopez sat back in his chair. "Damn," he said.

Lopez looked at Kai. He looked at me. "We have a back channel. There are people in the Authority who recognize how valuable the new portal could be. They know that a war will be expensive, will leave both sides impoverished, and the economic recovery will take at least a generation. So yes, they know that a war would be an expensive mistake. Unfortunately —they're not the ones who will make the final decision."

"And on our side?"

"The Executive Committee is all hard-liners now."

"Now?"

"This morning's attack on the Coordinator's residence changed a few minds. Because if they'd gotten Dolan, they'd have gone after the rest of the Executive Committee next." He put his coffee mug down. "And any other co-conspirators.. They have a long list."

"I assume I'm on it?"

"And Kai. And me. And Rottweiler and Collie and Poodle and all the other sonsabitches too. They'll tear down the whole operating structure of Praxis and replace it with know-nothing puppets. Their stupidity will kill people." He paused. "You actually have an escape clause."

"Huh?"

"You were contracted. If the Authority installs a puppet government, your contract is nullified. Your grandpa could pull some strings, claim you were an indenture, you didn't have a choice, blah blah blah, claim you were a political prisoner and demand that you be repatriated."

"And Kai?"

"Probably not. Not after they find out what happened to Frick and Frack. Whoever they were."

"I'm not going anywhere without him. I married him for better or worse."

"And he's stuck with you too."

"What is all this about?"

"We have a back channel. We've had quiet discussions for months. So far, it hasn't accomplished anything. It might be totally ineffective. But we have to try. We want to avoid a war. So do they. Well, some of them. Some of them think a war is necessary. They want to teach us a lesson."

I shook my head "There's only one lesson to be learned from war."

"And that is?"

"The only people who want war are people who've never been in one."

"Yes," he said. "I've been there." He did not explain. "What about you?"

"I'm an arbiter," I said. "I've known what happens when people behave stupidly. It's exhausting. Just listening to their justifications is exhausting. I wish the law would give me the right to slap the stupid out of them, but some of them, it's stupid all the way down. I would much prefer to stay in bed. With Kai. I'll make it simple. Even the best of wars has only one winner. Sex has two, even bad sex has two."

"It wasn't that bad," said Kai.

"I told you, I'll practice."

"As soon as possible."

Lopez waited patiently until we finished. "Can we please—?"

"No, we can't," I said to him. "I'm done. We're done. We almost got killed. We are definitely done. Both of us. You told me that I was only supposed to be a distraction. You used me. You used Kai. And now we're used up. We're innocent bystanders. Well, maybe just bystanders. Neither of us is that innocent, especially not after last night. But as far as I can tell, this conversation is just conversation. And coffee." I lifted my mug. "I could use a refill."

Lopez got up and retrieved the coffee pot. He refilled all three mugs and waited while Kai added sugar and milk. I drank mine black.

"Very well said, Dar. Very nice. But you're wrong." He looked across at me. "You're still useful."

NEGOTIATION

L opez said, "Read your contract. You don't get to quit."

"Who is my contract with? You? The Portal Authority? Coordinator Dolan? The Executive Committee? The government of Praxis? It doesn't matter. If you lose this war, there's no contract."

"We're not going to lose."

"I'd like to believe that."

"They want to negotiate."

"That's good news."

"They've got a very good negotiating team."

"I'd expect nothing less."

"Their senior negotiator is a legendary hard ass."

"Of course. Who'd they get?"

"Your grandfather."

I stared at him. "You're kidding."

"Is this my kidding face?"

I was getting a sick feeling in my stomach. "You're in trouble."

"Maybe. Maybe not."

"You'll need a senior negotiator who can't be bullied."

"We have one."

"Someone who can stand up to Senior Justice Ezra Ben Howell?"

Lopez nodded.

"Oh, who?"

"You."

The sick feeling spread from my stomach to my chest and all the way up to my throat. I choked for a moment.

"You haven't been paying attention," I said. "I lost to him. Every time."

"Not emotionally."

"That and a plastic dollar will rent a cup. The coffee costs extra."

"Listen to me, Dar. Ezz sent you away because he was tired of fighting you. You're smart and resourceful and young and inventive. You're also arrogant. But in this case, that's a virtue. Ezra Ben Howell is old and tired. Win or lose, he gets paid, so he doesn't have the emotional investment. But you'll fight him because you're here and you're Praxian. And . . ." He glanced meaningfully at Kai.

"There's an assumption in that sentence. No, two."

"Okay." He put his mug down. "'Splain me."

"First, there is an emotional investment for him. He's assuming I'll be your senior negotiator. So he sees it as one more chance to prove he's still better than me. That's been his pattern since he taught me chess. That man has to win, no matter what. He's terrified of losing. I've seen him lose a case. He usually ends up blaming the client for being stupid. And if he wins, it's the other side that was stupid for challenging him. He takes everything personally."

"So do you. What's the second assumption."

"That I'll join your team."

"We don't want you to join."

"No?"

"We want you to lead the team."

"Are you wearing your hearing aids? Did you miss the part where I said I lost to him?"

"I don't wear hearing aids. I have augments. And no, I did not miss that part. You only said you lost to him. You didn't say no." He leaned forward across the table. "You know his weaknesses. You know where to poke him. You know him better than anyone else on this entire planet. And . . ."

"What?"

"You want one more chance to beat him. And this time in an arena where it really counts."

I sat back in my chair.

The sick feeling that had been churning in

my gut started to resolve itself. It wasn't fear.

It was anger.

I took a long slow breath. "When do we start?"

ROUND ONE

T he first negotiating session was only four hours away. The local part of the negotiating committee was me, Lopez, and Kai. The other members of the committee were scattered across five stations. Coordinator Dolan would monitor the situation, but for negotiating purposes, I asked him to step back and not be present. The other side had decided that he was the enemy. I wanted them to see me as a mostly disinterested neutral party who had been drafted specifically for these meetings.

I gave my team simple instructions. "The first session is going to be where each side sizes the other up and states their demands, nothing else. Nobody talks except me. What I need from each of you right now is a very simple document. Two columns. Label one side 'Us,' the other side 'Them.'

"Then list down each side—and please don't be extravagant, that just wastes time, boil it down to the basics—what we demand, what they demand. Then list what we'll settle for, what they'll settle for. Somewhere in there is a solution—or the reason why no solution is possible. Don't worry about getting it right. What I want right now is a general sense of our starting position. I'll worry about consensus later. Any questions?"

Their questions were mostly about details and mechanics. But right now, all I needed was for them to look dispassionate and not react to anything that anyone said while we were live. Most of all, don't get emotional. We set up a side channel open only to us for all the things we needed to say that they shouldn't hear.

Just before we started, Kai leaned over to me. "Why am I here? I don't know anything—I mean, not about this."

I whispered back to him. "When we do the introductions, I'll introduce you as my special aide. Afterward, they're going to burrow through all their files looking up everything they can about every member of this team. When they get to you, they'll find out you're a trained assassin. I want them off-balance."

"Oh," he said. "Will that be part of my job —?"

"Oh god, I hope not. Once was bad enough."

And then the big screen opposite lit up. There were sixteen of them, but only Ezra

Ben Howell spoke. "Hello, Dar. Have you gained weight?"

"It's good to see you too, Grandpa."

"Please, I'm here in an official capacity. Call me Senior. That's my title."

"Yes, of course. And you will extend the same courtesy to me. The provisional government of Praxis has appointed me as their senior arbiter."

"We don't recognize the so-called 'Acting Government' as a legitimate negotiating body."

"Oh, okay. Well, then this session is over." I reached for the red button.

"Stop!" he commanded. "Do you want a war or not?"

I hesitated, my hand over the button. "First, of all, You have no authority to demand anything here. And secondly, if you do not recognize the authority of the government I represent, there is no basis for negotiation. Either we are equals at this table or we are not. And if we are not—then there is no basis for negotiation. So tell me right now, do you recognize my authority as granted by the provisional government of Praxis. Yes or no?"

He started to reply—

"Yes or no, Grandpa?"

He tried again—

"Yes or no!" I put my hand on the button.

He cleared his throat. He looked around to someone offscreen. He came back to me. "For the purposes of this negotiation, and only for this negotiation—"

"YES OR NO!"

"Yes, goddammit! Yes!"

"Let it be recorded that the negotiator for the Portal Authority and its allies has acknowledged the legitimacy of this committee's right to negotiate on behalf of the provisional government of Praxis, and therefore, by extension, the Portal Authority and its allies recognize the legitimacy of the provisional government of Praxis."

Round One. To the challenger.

We took a break.

ROUND TWO

The private channel filled up with comments ranging from "Well done!" to "Okay, now what?"

"First, what can we find out about all those suits sitting behind Grandpa? They're the real negotiating committee. Second—" I didn't have a second. "Second—keep up the good work."

More important, the point had been made.

They had conceded we were a government.

Maybe an antagonistic government, but by recognizing us as such, we were no longer a rebellion. This was critical—and if Grandpa's employers thought he had made a serious mistake, they were right.

If he had said, "We're trying to stop a war here, stop playing games, Dar," I would have had to back off. But the fact that he caved so quickly was either a ploy, or a signal that he knew how weak their position might be. Or . . . nah, that was

249

too easy a thought. But it was fun to think about anyway. Maybe he favored Praxis and was willing to lose this one—if I could make a compelling case.

But not my Grandpa. If I was an obnoxious arrogant jerk, it was because I'd learned it from him. Every conversation had always been a contest of wills—since the first time I refused to eat Grandma's over-salted cabbage rolls. So if he didn't like me, the feeling was more than mutual.

More likely, if he was willing to lose, it would be to keep me from coming back to Luna.

Even more likely, the Authority had to have chosen him specifically because they expected me to be the Chief Negotiator on this side. They expected him to grind me into the dirt.

Kai leaned over to me and whispered. "Dar?"

"Yes?"

"I can see it in your face. Remember your own words. Don't get emotional."

"You're right." I leaned back in my chair and closed my eyes. Breathe in for a five count, hold for five, breathe out for a five count, hold for five. Repeat five times.

I opened my eyes. The big screen came to life. We were on again.

Grandpa said, "All right, state your demands."

"No, you go first."

"You're the plaintiffs in this case—"

"Oh? I thought you were. Never mind. We'll flip for it." I pulled out a silver coin. A very rare Lunar dollar, with the face of Neil Armstrong on one side and the Eagle Lunar Lander on the other.

"I don't trust your coin," Grandpa said.

"You shouldn't. You gave it to me on my thirteenth birthday. Call it. Heads or tails."

"Heads."

"Too bad. Came up tails. You go first."

Grandpa did not look well. Being on the big screen only amplified the wrinkles, the age spots, the slight tremor in his left eyelid. If I could keep him angry, I could win the emotional battle. And if I won the emotional battle—

Grandpa shuffled some papers in front of him. "We demand the resignation of the so-called Provisional Government—"

"Not gonna happen. Next?"

"You could have let me finish my statement."

"Why? There's no point in you demanding things that we are not going to give. I'm tired of all this. I expect you are. You're going to get paid win or lose. You taught me too well, Grandpa. Do you want to cut to the chase now or should we continue to waste everybody's time and money doing the whole performance of negotiation before we finally get around to making the deal?"

"You're an ass," he said.

"You raised me, after Mom ran off with the vacuum salesman. If there's anything wrong with me, look in the mirror."

"You—the people you represent—they have a portal."

"So do you. The people you represent. It's to our benefit here and your benefit there to keep both portals open and functioning."

"Not stipulated."

"All right, let's get to the stipulations. Is it the Portal Authority's position that they should have the only access to Praxis?"

Grandpa looked to his papers. "That's not how I would phrase it, but yes. The corporation that opened this portal holds the sole license and is therefore granted sole access."

"Uh-huh. So a second portal—?"

"—is unauthorized."

"Nevertheless, it's here and it's open."

"But not yet functioning."

"Oh, it's functioning. We just haven't sent anything through." I added, "If the Portal Authority is willing to recognize the provisional government, the government of Praxis is willing to negotiate a new license. For both Portals."

"The Authority already owns the existing line."

"Yes, you do. We'll concede that. That's why the Authority had the right to close the portal unilaterally, effectively isolating Praxis from any contact with any other human inhabited world or station."

"We did not shut it down. The portal is still open."

"But all traffic to Praxis is being held at North Station or below and has been for sixteen hours. Ever since Coordinator Dolan rejected the ultimatum. So even though you can claim the portal is open, you have actually closed it. As you said, let's not play games here. Praxis reserves the right to protect its connection to all other human worlds and stations."

"You used the Authority's portals to transmit your portal mechanism. And if I understand portal mechanics—"

"If you do, you're the only one—"

He ignored me. "As I understand portal mechanics, the subspace connection is threaded through our line."

"Well, maybe. That part is theoretical. But you can test it any time. Shut down the portal."

Grandpa hesitated. He looked offscreen. Someone there must have shaken their head.

He came back to me.

"What do you want, Dar."

"Ah, I thought you'd never ask." I made a show of shuffling through some papers, as if I wasn't sure and had to remind myself. "Ah, here it is." I read from the paper. "The Provisional Government of the world known as Praxis recognizes the enormous investment that the Portal Authority has made developing this world. The Provisional Government of Praxis recognizes this debt and intends to honor it. Nevertheless—oh, wait—" I put that paper aside and searched through the others for the revised agreement. "Sorry, we were working late. I want to make sure I have the latest draft."

This was another trick I'd learned from Grandpa. Keep them distracted, make them think you're inefficient, waste their time. I glanced up. Grandpa had leaned back in his chair. He knew exactly what I was doing.

"Ah, here it, thank you for waiting." I focused on the text in front of me. "The Provisional Government of Praxis has been established to protect the rights and responsibilities of those who have settled here." I put the paper aside for a moment and stared directly at Grandpa.

"As you must know, once a person has gone shirtsleeve, there is no way for them to return to any other settlement or station, especially not Mars or Luna or Earth. The Portal Authority has very wisely restricted that access to protect the homeworlds against any microbial invasions from any offworld ecology. Did I get that right?"

I picked up the paper again. "Therefore, the Provisional Government has been established, did I read this part already, never mind, let me repeat, the Provisional Government has been established to protect the rights and responsibilities of those who have settled here. Therefore, the Portal Authority must recognize that the Provisional Government represents a viable population and that population must be recognized as an independent authority. Therefore, the Portal Authority must renegotiate its agreements accordingly, recognizing the authority of the Provisional Government to speak for the permanent settlers of Praxis." I put the paper down. "Is that clear?"

Grandpa waved it away. "I thought we had already addressed that."

"Well, no. We want a formal recognition of the Provisional Government. After that, I am authorized to negotiate licensing terms for both portals."

Grandpa pursed his lips. He could see the logic. But the people behind him did not look happy. And whoever was making faces at him offscreen was probably gesticulating wildly, making prearranged signals and frantic gestures, probably even putting up notes on giant screens. Grandpa's attention had been flickering off to the side enough times that he looked like he was trying to keep up with instructions.

Abruptly, Grandpa came back to me. "Dar, that was very nicely written. My compliments. But what you are asking is for the Portal Authority to give up . . . well, it's authority. What shall we call it then? The Portal But Only If Praxis

Gives Permission."

"That's a little wordy," I said. "But accurate. How about we simply call it Portal Access?"

Grandpa sat back in his chair. I recognized that posture. He was about to say that the negotiation was over.

So I sat back in my chair too.

"We're trying to avoid a war," he said.

"Yes, we are. And if the Authority intends to go to war, I am obligated to point out just how expensive it could be."

"Really?"

"There are several reasons why it would be inadvisable. First of all, as you probably know, the new Portal Station is on the seacoast. And as you and I both know, the Authority is assembling an invasion force at the North Dakota Portal Access. All your puppet masters need to do, Grandpa, is lose patience with this process and they'll start moving the invasion force across. Tanks and drones and bots and whatever other machines they can muster. You don't need to confirm it. We have pictures from commercial satellites. Very impressive. But—"

He waited.

"—the moment that first unauthorized vehicle comes through that portal, the Provisional Government of Praxis is prepared to open the floodgates. Literally. Your invasion force will be met by a wall of seawater. In fact, at this time of year, there will probably be some large chunks of ice in the flood. Are your machines submersible? Based on the pictures we've seen, they aren't."

Grandpa only had two expressions. Frown and Darker Frown. But now his expression changed. This one I'd never seen before. Darkest Frown.

"That would be a violation of—"

"No, it wouldn't. You're only sending machines. You're unwilling to send personnel, because they'd have to wear bio-armor. If your simulations are any good, you already expect to lose a third of them, or at least not be able to bring them back. But that's part of your figuring too. If the Authority can establish a permanent military force here, then recognition of the government is unnecessary. Correct so far?"

"I need to pee," said Grandpa. "Give me a five-minute recess." The screen went blank.

"He needed to pee like I need . . . hm, that's odd. I don't need anything, do I?" I glanced to Kai. "How'd I do?"

"I'm impressed. But then—I said that last night, didn't I?"

Lopez poked my left side. "Does his eye always twitch like that?"

"I don't know. I've never pushed him this hard. But then again, I never had a negotiation like this."

I turned to the rest of the negotiating committee. "Okay, tell me who all those people in the background are."

ROUND THREE

The reports flickered up on my screen. These are not negotiators. Not in the sense that they were there to negotiate. All those suits were corporate lawyers. Interesting.

It meant one thing for sure—the corporations that owned Portal Authority were extremely interested in the outcome of these talks. Whatever Grandpa intended, he was at the service of their agenda.

A corporation only has one agenda. Profit. And sometimes profit without honor. Because profit is always more useful than honor.

Right on schedule, the screen lit up and Grandpa was back. He looked a lot calmer.

"All right," he said. "So you can stall an invasion. You can't stop it permanently."

"No, we can't."

"So, all you're doing is stalling now."

"Why do you say that?"

"Praxis has no troops. You can't counter-attack."

"Oh. Damn. Yes. I forgot about that. Wait. I think we made some notes about that too. Oh, yes, here it is—" I held the paper up in front of me and pretended to frown at it—"

"Stop wasting my time, Dar. I taught you that trick."

"Yes, you did. Thank you, Grandpa." I put the paper down. "I was wondering how long it would take before you called me out on it." I swiveled in my chair and called to an imaginary audience. "How long did we go? Who won the pool?"

I turned back to Grandpa. It was time to get serious. "Okay, Senior Ezra Ben Howell, here's what you need to know. We have opened all of our airlocks on this side to the Praxis biosphere." I was lying, yes, but they needed to hear that it was possible. Even probable.

I pushed on. "I don't know what safety precautions anyone has taken in North Dakota, maybe it'll be enough, we didn't have a chance to test them or upgrade them or see if they could still function as zero-defect seals. So if the Portal Authority attempts to enter this planet, they might be exposing Earth's atmosphere to an alien ecology. Maybe they should check their safeguards. Of course, if confidence isn't green —"

Grandpa hesitated. "I should have

strangled you in your crib."

"Yes, that was your second mistake. Your first was the way you raised my mother. Shall we focus on this situation first?"

"It's still a stall," he said.

"Yes. But . . ." I paused. "No. Tell you what. Let's take a break. And your people, all those scurrying little cockroaches in their cute little uniforms—have them run some economic situations. What happens to the Portal Authority if Praxis stays offline for six months. Or eighteen months. Or forever. What happens to their investment then. How do you think the shareholders will respond?"

"You fight dirty."

"No, I fight to win. You taught me that."

I closed the channel.

PAUSE

I turned to Lopez. "Don't congratulate me. We didn't win."

"But we didn't lose," he said.

"It depends on their numbers. The Corporations that own the Portal Authority have a bad habit. They're greedy. So they overextend themselves. I'm betting they're not in the strongest financial position. Too many mining worlds are producing too much raw material. If those prices get too low, the return is insufficient to justify the investment. Shutting down a mining operation is also expensive. Reopening it later on is even more expensive. All that equipment, if it isn't running it's not only useless, it depreciates. And then there's the human cost too, hiring, training, guarantees, bonuses, pensions—if there's no income to offset it, it's a drain. Our single sole advantage, if they're smart enough to recognize it, is that a license means we take over the support systems here. We represent a chance to cut their losses."

Lopez studied me for a long moment. "You did your research, didn't you?"

"I grew up on Luna, the biggest damn mining colony in the entire solar system. Before the portals, we had the lowest gravity well in the system. And a lot closer than the asteroid belt. We had the best smelters too. After the portals, we built more. Nobody else had to. Nobody else wanted to make the investment. That's how Luna got rich. You don't grow up in Turtledome without learning the business. Why do you think Grandpa settled there."

"Oh," he said.

I pointed at the screen. "If they do their homework, they'll come back tomorrow with a licensing agreement. If not—I might have to get creative."

"This wasn't creative?"

"I didn't fire the big gun, no."

"You have one?"

"No. But I can lie convincingly."

"Please don't tell me.

"I wasn't planning on it."

Lopez started to rise. He stopped himself. "Just one more thing—"

"What?"

"Except for when you shuffled through those papers, you never put your hands on the table. What was that about? Was that one of your body language trick?"

"No," I said. "I was just holding Kai's hand. That's what I do whenever I get . . . whatever."

EVENING

We conferred with Dolan and his advisors.

We decompressed. We calmed ourselves. We had sandwiches.

We debriefed. All of us. Lopez and all the rest of the negotiating committee. Dolan and his advisors added their thoughts.

We reviewed everything.

What worked? What didn't work? What do we have to watch in the future?

We discussed plans, opportunities, alternatives. Plan B. Plan C. Plan R.

And finally, in exhaustion, we called it a night.

Kai and I sat in a hot tub that someone had thoughtfully set up for us and just looked at each other.

Eventually we climbed out. We put on robes. We ate clam chowder and Caesar's salad. And hot bread.

We reviewed again, this time the personal stuff. We finished with coffee and cake.

We went to bed. We held onto each other, just Kai and me. Finally we slept.

We tried to sleep. I stared at the ceiling and reviewed every mistake I thought I'd made, every misstep, every miscalculation.

Grandpa was probably doing the same. I hoped he was as uncomfortable as I was.

We were not in a strong position. They could close off both portals, write us off, and forget about us. Our only chance was to convince them that it was better for them to keep us connected.

It would be better for us too, but I doubted that they cared about that.

Maybe Grandpa did.

He'd taught me that the only lasting resolution to any conflict was to find a way to make it a win-win.

And maybe, but this was a very slim hope, but maybe he still cared enough about me that he wouldn't let them shut down the portal.

But I couldn't count on that, could I?

NEXT

"All right, what do we know from this first meeting?"

Silence around the table. Nobody wanted to be the first to speak.

I couldn't blame them—this many people in a meeting, the meeting was going to have a terrible signal-to-noise ratio. The more people in the room, the less likely the decision would be definitive.

This was the primary negotiating committee and the additional team of offscreen observers and advisors. We assumed the other side had at least as many, probably more, and very likely a few intelligence engines as well. That might be their weakness. Depending on the logic of the engines was a sure way to miss the human aspect of any negotiation.

The painful silence continued.

Finally, Lopez looked to Kai and nodded.

Kai said, "Your Grandpa isn't running the

show."

"Yes," I said. "Who is?"

Kai looked to Lopez then back to me. "The guy at the end. The skinny little weasel with the tablet, the one who doesn't look up. His name is Crow. He just keeps typing like he's working on his first novel."

"And your Grandfather keeps looking offscreen," said Lopez. "Probably Crow's notes. I don't think they're giving him guidance. They're giving him orders. His body language is off. He's nervous about something."

"I agree," I said. "He's at odds with the rest of the committee."

They all looked at me, waiting for me to go on.

"I know Grandpa. He doesn't listen well. He makes up his mind and bulls ahead regardless of anyone's advice. He's always certain he knows better. He wants—no, he needs to beat me. I'm not sure what the rest of the committee wants."

Dolan, sitting at his own table, now on the screen, raised his hand. "May I?"

"Please."

"We've been running a separate simulation of their side, including the intelligence engines. The logic of the situation is to license both portals and double the amount of traffic. We could negotiate that agreement in less than an hour. But there's an anomaly—"

"Arbiter Ezra Ben Howell."

Dolan nodded. "He's at odds with the logic."

I nodded agreement. I let go of Kai's hand and put my palms flat on the table. "I think we are at a cusp. Not ours, theirs. But ours as well. Grandpa is acting like he wants a war. Is that to intimidate us? Maybe. Or maybe he wants to justify the war? I don't know. Is there a personal agenda in there? Possibly. Grandpa wants me off Luna. He might pretend otherwise, but—and I'm sorry if this sounds arrogant, because it is—I have to believe he sees me as a threat, so he can't achieve satisfaction until he establishes some kind of dominance over me.

"So, what is our response to that? We stall. We keep the negotiations going for as long as possible."

"Until—?" asked Dolan.

"Until his bosses get tired and fire him."

"Do you really think they'll fire him?"

"How many CEOs does a corporation go through in a decade? There's no loyalty there. Only—Grandpa has never been fired. Never that I know of. I don't know how he'll take it. Maybe he'll sue them for breach of contract. No, there's no maybe. He will. But until then—"

"How long?" said Dolan.

"How long can we hold out? Or how long can they? They have the resources, we don't. But they have a problem we don't have."

"Please . . . ?"

"Run the numbers. How much money are they losing every day with the portals closed? How much per week? Month? How long can they continue the shutdown before it becomes financially painful? That's when they get desperate. They have to be hoping that we'll get desperate first."

Dolan nodded. He looked around the table, then back to me. "So as I see it, correct me if I'm wrong—we have to hope our beagle is worse than their beagle."

"If this were an ordinary negotiation, I'd say that you're correct."

"And if this is not ordinary . . . ?"

"Then the question is, who's going to fire their beagle first?"

Dolan looked across to me. "It'll have to be them. You're the only beagle we have."

"That's my take on it, yes." I added, "And I'm pretty sure they've figured it out too."

ROUND FOUR

The screen came to life.

Grandpa wasn't there.

Instead, it was Crow. The skinny little weasel. Fitted suit. Hair cut short in an industrial haircut. A little too clean. He looked manufactured.

"Where's Grandpa—Arbiter Ezra Ben Howell?"

"I'm sorry," he said. "Arbiter Howell resigned last night."

"Resigned or fired?"

"Does it matter?"

"Actually, yes. He's my grandfather, and despite the fact that we have never been on the same side of an argument, legal or otherwise, he's still my grandfather and I do have some familial loyalty. Not much, but enough to ask. Resigned or fired?"

Crow hesitated.

"And yes," I continued, "It will have an

effect on these negotiations. It might speed them up. Especially if you're honest with me."

Crow still didn't answer. My bad. I had him off balance—useful only to a certain point in any negotiation. But if anyone is ever going to resolve anything, the other side has to feel confidence in the outcome. No lasting deal was ever built on resentment.

So I said, "Please, we all want this settled. We have survival needs. You have financial obligations. We can make a deal here, one that benefits both positions. But it has to be based on honesty and respect. So please, tell me, resigned or fired?

Crow took a breath. "We asked him to step aside. He refused."

"That sounds like Grandpa."

"We exercised the termination clause in his contract."

"So, fired."

"He is no longer employed by the Portal Authority," said Crow. "And . . . his contract as a senior arbiter for Turtledome will not be renewed when it expires at the end of the year."

"That might be dangerous. The position at Turtledome was Luna's way of keeping Grandpa sidelined, so he wouldn't go into politics."

"Possibly. But the Turtledome expansion has been approved, including a new transit line, so the duties of an arbiter will have to be expanded. As I understand it, the authority is looking for someone younger, but with experience. You would be qualified. In fact, your name was mentioned more than once." He studied me, waiting for my answer.

"Um—stop. Please. This conversation is inappropriate for these negotiations. It could almost be considered an offer of a bribe. But yes, in the interests of moving past this, and staying focused on the issues on this table, you may take this back to whoever needs to hear it. If and when we conclude this negotiation, we can have any other conversation they wish to initiate, but only if my current employers are satisfied that we have achieved our goals here."

"We expected nothing less from you. It is why you have been so highly recommended."

"And the icing on that cake is the animosity between me and Grandpa, right? Because if you really want to hurt him, appointing me to his old job would do it. And if it's an expanded authority, well let's just pour some more salt into that wound. Just how much did the old bastard piss you off?"

Now it was Crow's turn to demur. "Let's have that discussion another time. Perhaps over dinner when you return to Luna?"

"Perhaps." I looked around at the people at my side of the table, at their uncertain expressions. Below the table, where Crow couldn't see it, I held my hand out, palm down, and made a stay calm gesture.

I looked back to Crow. "So you really want to punish the old bastard, right? Because he wasn't doing what you wanted and needed in these negotiations, right? You didn't waste any time in kicking him to the curb. Do you still have curbs? Do you even know what a curb is? Never mind. And you want me to consider taking his old job? For employers with no loyalty at all?"

"Your grandfather has a generous severance package."

"That's not the point. You hired him and then you didn't trust him to do what you want. So either he's a fool, or you people are the bigger fools—"

"We want to settle this. He didn't."

"Of course, he didn't. He wanted to beat me. He needed to beat me. You took that away from him."

"What we want is a settlement. He did not."

"You think I didn't know that? This negotiating committee, representing the legally recognized Provisional Government of Praxis also knew it. Regardless of who sits on your side of the table, we have been prepared to continue these talks for as long as necessary until someone over there is willing to say what you just said. We want a settlement too."

Crow stopped. He looked around at the members of his negotiating team. Several of them nodded.

On our side, nobody said anything—then, below the table, Kai grabbed my hand and held it. Lopez moved close to me on the left.

I came to life, shaking them both off.

"All right, Let's finish this. Here's what we want. You'll open your portal, we'll open ours. Portal Authority gets exclusive license to both. But only seven years, then we renegotiate the terms to mutual benefit, and recognizing our right to determine our own trading partners. Fair enough? You get the right to attempt seven outbound portals here on Praxis. Praxis gets 67% ownership and management rights for staging. We guarantee no acts of war. So do you. Failure to uphold any part of this contract, judged by a panel of independent arbiters, we choose one, you choose one, the chosen arbiters choose the third—failure to uphold any part of this contract and you forfeit all rights, responsibilities, and claims of ownership. If you want to make a counteroffer, we'll review it, but if it's not a win-win for both sides, we're not interested. Oh, and most important, you must recognize the Provisional Government here as the sole authority for Praxis and withdraw all personnel that this government deems hostile. No, put down your hand. No questions."

I didn't even wait for him to acknowledge. I logged off.

VICTORY?

Before I could say anything, Kai grabbed me in a hug and held me tight.

After a moment, I pulled away. "They fired him a lot faster than I expected. Maybe they're smarter than we thought. And if they are, we're in trouble. We're going to have to hold any agreements up to the light to look for secret messages before we sign anything."

"This is about your grandfather, isn't it?"

I looked to Lopez, to Kai, and all the others. "He hated me." I had to correct myself, "Okay, maybe he didn't hate me. He just disliked dealing with me. And the feeling was mutual. But he was still my grandfather. Take it or leave it." And after that, when I had finished wiping my eyes, I came up in the middle of a circle of concerned faces.

"But you beat him," Lopez said. "That's what this was really about, wasn't it?"

"No. This was about Praxis. It was always about Praxis. And if I had to beat him to win for Praxis, then . . . okay, I had to beat him. They chose him deliberately. They thought it would give them an advantage, but it didn't, so they pulled him. If he's hurt, it's on them. Not me. I didn't want to hurt him—but they wanted to hurt us. Because that's how this kind of corporate shenanigans work. When using Grandpa didn't work, they went to their next step, trying to bribe me. And when that didn't work, they still didn't negotiate. Not a real negotiation where each side has something the other wants or needs, because they don't know how. They've never known how. It's not in their mindset. The next trick? They're going to make a counteroffer that erases everything we want. Oh, it'll look good, but it'll be the same kind of trap. And that's why we can't trust them. Ever. And I'm sorry I have to say that and even sorrier that I have to think that way, but . . . I spent too many years at law school to think any other way."

Lopez put a hand on my shoulder.

He meant to be reassuring, but I shrugged it away. "No, it's all right. I'm fine," I lied. I looked around to all of them. "I'm sorry that I got emotional. I told you not to, and then I didn't listen to myself. I didn't follow the plan, our very meticulous plan. We were going to walk them step by step down the primrose path—"

"We don't have any primroses here," said Kai. "They all died."

"Well, maybe some in the greenhouse,"

said Lopez. "I can check"

"It's a metaphor, a goddamned metaphor. Charles Fucking Darwin on a stick! Is everyone on this damn planet illiterate?"

"Most of us haven't had much time for reading."

"Obviously."

Somebody pushed a cup of hot tea into my hands, a young man, I didn't remember his name. "For what it's worth, Arbiter, we think you did great. You laid it out fairly."

"Thank you. And thank you for the tea."

Lopez pointed at the screen wall. "Well, we've given them an ultimatum. They'll either accept it or reject it—"

"Or annotate it for changes. If they really want a settlement, it'll be minor things, most of which we'll grudgingly accept to give them some sense of victory. They have reputations too. They can't look like they caved in. We have to give them something."

"What do you think?" asked Lopez.

"I don't know—I just don't." I sipped at the tea.

When I finished, Kai took the cup from my hands and put it on the table. "I think you're done for today. Come on, I'll take you home."

GRANDPA

The phone chimed.

It was Grandpa. He looked haggard.

"Hello."

He nodded in reply.

"Congratulations."

I shook my head. "Why?"

"You won."

"No, I didn't."

"You beat me. And if you beat me, you beat them."

"You don't know that."

"Yes, I do. I'm not stupid. I also know you turned down their transparent attempt to bribe you."

"I learned that from you. If you accept a bribe, any bribe, no matter how much, then they own you forever."

Grandpa said, "You learned more than that from me. You learned how to be a royal pain in the ass."

"I should thank you for that?"

"Yes, you should. You were vulnerable. I taught you how to survive. In a world of sharks, you have to be the bigger shark." He hesitated, his face softened, another expression I'd never seen before. "After your mom left, I knew I couldn't protect you. Not from all the hurts that life would throw at you. So I remember, I had to . . . I had to make a very tough decision, Dar. I had to make you stronger and harder than anyone and everyone. There wasn't any room for softness or weakness or . . . anything. Maybe I was wrong, but I didn't know any other way. And today . . . well, you proved I was right. Well, partially right. So, I got that part of my job done, and I suppose I should be proud of you. You did good."

"I damaged your reputation for never losing."

He shook his head. "Not much. Maybe you missed it, but the real conversation down here is about the nature of independence. You can't own a planet. You can't own people. I don't know if anybody will listen, human beings don't listen, don't learn, but I'm planning to write a book about it anyway. That's why I called."

"I thought you called to congratulate me."

"Well, that, yes. But there's always an agenda. You know that. I just wanted to ask your permission to quote you in my report."

"You don't have to ask. It's all public

record."

"Yes, it is. But you and I—we have to be on the same side."

"Why?"

"Because I don't have the energy to fight you again, you idiot."

"Neither do I, and you're the bigger idiot for accepting that job."

"They paid me well."

"Not enough. You still lost."

"Oh, yes they did. I made sure of that. And I didn't lose. It was a strategic withdrawal. On their part. I still had a few arguments to make, a couple issues to raise, we would have put on a good show, but your outburst scared them. Not my fault. Theirs. There isn't a pair of testicles in the whole committee. Well, maybe Crow."

"He's not stupid."

"No, he isn't. But he doesn't have the heart for a long fight. That was your best advantage. One more thing. Have you gone shirtsleeve?"

"Not yet."

"Good. I hope to see you again when you come back to Luna. Even if it's only for a visit."

"I love you too, Grandpa."

He waved it away. But was that a hint of a smile before he logged off?

ENDGAME

I was lying awake in bed, staring at the ceiling again. Kai sat on a chair opposite, drinking tea and listening to music, deliberately leaving me alone until I was ready to talk. Or cuddle. Or take another bath. Or whatever.

The phone chimed.

I got out of bed and crossed to the table. The screen blinked to life.

It was Coordinator Dolan.

Kai took off his headphones and put down his cup of tea. He came and sat beside me.

"I hear you heard from your grandfather."

"There are no secrets here, are there?"

"Not on this level, no. I heard he offered his congratulations. Let me offer mine."

"We still have a long way to go. They're coming back to the table tomorrow."

"Your grandfather didn't tell you? Well, he couldn't know. Not yet. They accepted our terms —your terms."

"Wait. What? Really?"

"In principle, yes. They sent a note."

"Not to me."

"Of course not. You're not the Coordinator. They want to recognize the government of Praxis."

"Oh, then I should be congratulating you."

"On the contrary. They've conceded our right to negotiate as a government. We won the moment. You made recognition essential to the negotiation." He continued, "The language still has to be worked out, and there are some mechanical details, like you predicted, but those will be worked out by our respective teams."

"Ah, that's where they'll find a place to stick it to us."

"Maybe. We'll burn that bridge when we get to it. But I think they're serious."

"Why?"

"Because they want to know when we can schedule a formal ceremony. I told them that as soon as they publicly acknowledge that Praxis is now self-governing and that they are ready to recognize the authority of the provisional government, then both sides can ratify a treaty. Your language. And they agreed. They're working on the documents now. You do realize, this sets a precedent. Not just for the Authority, but for every other portal world and any other agency that deals with them. You may have started a series of revolutions. Was that your hidden agenda?"

"It never occurred to me," I said, blank-faced.

"Of course. Why would I ever suspect a lawyer of having a hidden agenda? Oh, there is one other thing—" He took a breath. He straightened, a signal that he was now speaking officially.

I waited for him to continue.

"Speaking as Coordinator, and with the approval of the Executive Committee, the Government of Praxis would like to offer you a position in the new administration."

"I think I might have a counteroffer. . . ." I said, grinning.

He wasn't amused. "We'll match it and surpass it."

"Okay," I said. "I will be proud to be your senior arbiter."

"Um, no. Well, only if you don't accept this job."

"What?"

"Ambassador to Earth." He pointed to Kai, "Oh, and your husband too. He'll be your deputy."

APPENDIX

◆ ◆ ◆

PROPOSED CONSTITUTION FOR PRAXIS

PREAMBLE
We the undersigned, in order to establish a fair set of agreements by which to govern ourselves, to establish justice, ensure domestic tranquility, provide for the common defense, and promote the well-being of all participants, do ordain and establish this Constitution for the planet Praxis.

PURPOSE
The purpose of this government is to serve the needs of all people living under its jurisdiction. This shall include any and all citizens as well as any and all who have not yet accepted the rights and responsibilities of citizenship.

CITIZENSHIP
Any and all persons signatory to this agreement shall be considered full citizens, guaranteed

all rights and privileges guaranteed by this Constitution.

Citizenship shall be limited to those individuals who can demonstrate a fundamental understanding of the workings of this government, including but not limited to the essential guarantees of freedom of speech and expression, the rights and responsibilities of citizens, the rights and responsibilities of voting, and the rights and responsibilities of taxation as a function of representation.

Any and all individuals reaching the age of thirteen years shall have the right and responsibility to become a signatory to this agreement and by the act of signing, shall become full citizens as defined by this Constitution, and by the act of signing shall be due all rights of citizenship as well as all the responsibilities of citizenship, including but not limited to all agreements included herein, but especially the right to participate in any and all elections.

All citizens may vote in all elections, without restriction. It is the responsibility of federal, state, and local authorities to provide access to all polling services. Failure of any person entrusted with the responsibility of providing polling services shall be considered a criminal act and shall result in, but not limited to, immediate removal from any and all elected and/or appointed offices or positions.

Only residents of a local jurisdiction may vote in that jurisdiction's elections. Only residents of a state's jurisdiction may vote in that state's elections.

Only citizens shall be eligible to hold any office or positions established under the authority of this Constitution. No person shall hold any office in any jurisdiction without having been a full resident of that jurisdiction for at least three years.

Any and all persons living under the jurisdiction of this Constitution, who have not become signatory citizens, shall still be guaranteed all rights and privileges and responsibilities listed herein, excepting the right to vote or hold office at any level of government authority.

No person convicted of a felony may hold any elected or appointed office or position at any level of government including, but not limited to federal, state, or local positions. Without exception convicted felons shall be permanently ineligible to hold any office created under this jurisdiction.

Any and all persons convicted of a felony

under the jurisdiction of this Constitution shall have their citizenship suspended for a period not less than seven years, such suspension not to be rescinded without a legislative pardon granted by a two-thirds majority of Congress. The Congress may grant such pardons as they deem appropriate. The Executive Committee may also submit to the legislature the names of individuals they deem worthy of legislative pardon.

ELECTIONS
Without exception, Election Day shall be a national holiday, occurring on the first Tuesday following the first Monday of the next to last month of the year. Special and local elections shall also be full holidays in their specific jurisdictions.

Without exception, all elections will be federally funded. All qualified candidates, polling 5% or better, shall be entitled to equal funding of their campaigns. All candidates shall have equal representation in all media.

Without exception, the media shall have the responsibility of presenting all candidates in equal measure. The media shall have the responsibility of examining the practicality and the specific consequences of any action that any candidate proposes.

No votes shall be cast in any electronic medium where there is no physical record of that vote. All votes shall be cast in a physical form to guarantee the security of a fair recount, where one is needed or requested.

All votes shall be cast according to ranked preferences:
If, for example, there are three candidates for a specific office, the voter shall mark first, second, and third choices. The voter shall also have the opportunity of ranking candidates as a zero, meaning that candidate will receive no vote from this ballot.

The first tally of the votes will count all the first-place votes.

The second tally will add all the second-place votes.

The third tally will add all the third-place votes.
And so on, up until the fifth tally. This system shall not be expanded beyond a fifth level of votes. The candidate receiving the most votes from all the tallies wins the election.

This method of counting allows all parties to have representation while still guaranteeing that the candidate receiving a majority endorsement from all the voters will win the election.

Without exception, any person, organization, or corporation engaging in any illegal or inappropriate conduct designed to influence any public election shall be liable to all necessary consequences, including but not limited to the loss of citizenship and the ability to participate in all further elections on any level.

BRANCHES OF GOVERNMENT
Only citizens shall serve in any position of government, including, but not limited to federal, state, and local positions. Only citizens may vote in elections.

Supreme Court
Nominations for the Supreme Court will be made by the Executive Committee and approved by a majority vote of the Legislature.

There shall be one Supreme Court Justice for every Legislative District.

The Executive Committee shall have the responsibility of nominating Justices to fill vacancies on the Supreme Court. The Legislature shall have the responsibility of interviewing all judicial candidates and shall further have the responsibility of approving or rejecting the nomination of said candidate.

No more than one Justice may be appointed per Legislative term. If any seat goes unfilled, the Deputy Justice for that district will serve until an appointment is made by the Executive Committee and approved by the Congress.

All appointments to the Supreme Court made by the Executive Committee, must be considered an immediate priority and voted on by the Legislature, without exception.

No individual may be nominated for a seat on the Supreme Court without first having served seven years or more in active practice of law and seven years or more in an active judicial position.

The Supreme Court shall consist of an odd number of justices, with one justice appointed for each defined Legislative District, with appropriate and necessary consideration given first to candidates from the district they will represent. Candidates not from that district may be considered only when no suitable candidates from that district are available.

In any situation where there exists only an even number of districts, a new Chief Justice shall be appointed by the Executive Committee, not representing any specific district.

Supreme Court justices shall serve a term of

seven years. No person may serve more than two terms on the Supreme Court without the authorization of a two-thirds majority of the Legislature.

Legislature

Praxis shall have a single legislative body, comprised of two representatives from each district. The requirements for a representative are:

Representatives must be citizens.

Representatives must be 25 years or older.

Representative candidates must have lived at least 3 years in their district.

Representative candidates must have served at least 3 years as a deputy or any higher position in any legislative body.

Any individual attempting to stall the workings of Legislature by filibuster will be dragged from his office and staked to an anthill at the earliest possible opportunity. If there are no anthills readily available, the individual may be expelled from Legislature by 60% of the voting members, or by a 60% majority vote of the voters in their district.

Executive Committee

There will be an Administrator for each of the following departments:

Defense

The Executive Committee shall have the responsibility of appointing an Administrator of Defense and determining the duties and responsibilities of the Administrator of Defense.

Economy

The Executive Committee shall have the responsibility of appointing an Administrator of the Economy and determining the duties and responsibilities of the Administrator of the Economy.

The Administrator of the Economy shall have as their primary duty, the management of the MINIMUM BASIC WAGE, as follows:

Because the greatest affliction affecting any economy is poverty, the following preventative measures shall be a necessary agreement of all citizens.

The Economic Committee shall have as a primary responsibility, the annual determination of the cost of living for all declared constituencies, townships, counties, states, and other agencies.

The Minimum Basic Wage shall be set annually as the cost of living for any specific jurisdiction plus 25%. Any and all citizens who do not have sufficient employment shall be eligible to receive the Minimum Basic Wage from the public trust. Sufficient income shall be defined as equal or more than Minimum Basic Wage.

The Minimum Basic Wage shall apply to all employments under this jurisdiction, regardless of any individual's age, sex, gender, state of citizenship, or other arbitrarily defined class.

No prohibitive conditions may be attached to any individual's right to a sustainable income. Individuals will have the inalienable right to sue for redress for damages suffered.

As an inducement to encourage citizenship, all persons who become full citizens shall have their Minimum Basic Wage raised by 15%.

TAXATION
Because the second greatest affliction affecting any economy is the inordinate distribution of wealth, inevitably creating the affliction of poverty, the following preventative measures shall be a necessary agreement of all citizens.

Taxation on income shall only begin when an individual is earning Minimum Basic Wage plus

100% of Minimum Basic Wage.

Based on the idea that those who benefit the most from participation in the economy should carry the greatest share of its maintenance, all taxes will be progressive, but not to exceed 90% of annual income.

All incomes, regardless of citizenship, within jurisdiction this shall be capped at 1000% of the Minimum Basic Wage. Any individual receiving income over that cap, from any source not part of this jurisdiction shall have the choice of forfeiting either that income or their citizenship.

Education

The Executive Committee shall have the responsibility of appointing an Administrator of Education and determining the duties and responsibilities of the Administrator of Education.

The Administrator of Education shall have as their primary duty, the encouragement of a well-educated and well-informed populace, as follows:

Access to education is a fundamental right. The Department of Education will guarantee that all people living under the jurisdiction of these agreements shall have unlimited and free access to all educational opportunities.

Access to education is also a corresponding responsibility for all educators to provide information that is credible, reliable, and verifiable through independent means.

Continuing Education is a fundamental strength of a healthy society. The government is prohibited from imposing any limits on any person's right to education.

All federal, state, and local educational opportunities shall be funded from the Public Trust. Additional educational opportunities may receive funding by the Public Trust as deemed appropriate by the Executive Committee of the Public Trust.

Exterior
The Executive Committee shall have the responsibility of appointing an Administrator of the Exterior and determining the duties and responsibilities of the Administrator of the Exterior.

The Department of the Exterior will monitor and maintain safe and healthy living conditions for all people who live in the native environments of Praxis.

Health

The Executive Committee shall have the responsibility of appointing an Administrator of Health and determining the duties and responsibilities of the Administrator of Health.

The Administrator of Education shall have as their primary duty, the encouragement of a healthy population, as follows:

Access to health care is a fundamental right. The Department of Health will guarantee that all people living under the jurisdiction of these agreements shall have unlimited and free access to all health care opportunities.

Access to health care is also a corresponding responsibility for all providers to deliver necessary services in a timely and appropriate manner, without regard for any distinctions or circumstances unrelated to health care.

Interior

The Executive Committee shall have the responsibility of appointing an Administrator of the Interior and determining the duties and responsibilities of the Administrator of the Interior.

The Department of the Interior will monitor and maintain safe and healthy living conditions for all people who live within environments separated from the exterior conditions of Praxis.

State
The Executive Committee shall have the responsibility of appointing an Administrator of State and determining the duties and responsibilities of the Administrator of State.

Trade
The Executive Committee shall have the responsibility of appointing an Administrator of Trade and determining the duties and responsibilities of the Administrator of Trade.

Transportation
The Executive Committee shall have the responsibility of appointing an Administrator of Transportation and determining the duties and responsibilities of the Administrator of Transportation.

Treasury
The Executive Committee shall have the responsibility of appointing an Administrator of the Treasury and determining the duties and responsibilities of the Administrator of the Treasury.

The Department of the Treasury shall be responsible for managing all financial responsibilities of the government that are not managed by The Public Trust.

The Department of the Treasury shall be responsible for issuing the legal currency of the government.

The Department of the Treasury shall be responsible for managing the Federal Reserve and setting the prime interest rate for loans.

The Department of the Treasury shall be responsible for setting the interest rates for all public and private loans.

No interest rate shall be set higher than 10% without the specific authorization of the Executive Committee and the Congress.

JUSTICE
The Executive Committee shall have the responsibility of appointing an Administrator of Justice and determining the duties and responsibilities of the Administrator of Justice.

The Administrator of Justice shall manage and maintain a Department of Justice, responsible for the fair and equal application of all laws authorized by this Constitution.
No person, subject to the jurisdiction of this government shall be denied due process. Every person or persons living under the jurisdiction

of this government shall have the right to a fair and just trial, shall have the right to examine all evidence against them, shall have the right to confront their accusers and all accusations against them in a court of law, shall be presumed innocent until proven guilty by a compelling demonstration of evidence in a court of law.

All cases shall be resolved within 18 months. If the case has not been heard in 18 months, judgment may be issued based on entered evidence. If there is no compelling evidence, the case may be dismissed.

Where appropriate, the presiding judge may grant a single extension of another 18 months. There shall be no extensions beyond that.

In order to limit the use of delaying tactics, litigants shall have the right of appeal, but shall be limited to only three appeals, excepting only those situations where a presiding judge is willing to make an exception.

PUBLIC TRUST
The Executive Committee shall have the responsibility of appointing an Administrator of the Public Trust and determining the duties and responsibilities of the Administrator of the Public Trust.

The Public Trust shall be established as an independent agency of this government.

It shall be responsible for managing any and all disbursements to individuals, including but not limited to Minimum Basic Wage, Disability, Health Care, and related costs.

No individual may serve as an Administrator or Deputy Administrator until they have served a minimum of seven years in that specific department.

The Administrators shall select from among themselves, an Executive who will function as Coordinator. The Deputy Administrator of that department will then serve as an Administrator.

If the Administrators are unable to select a Coordinator after seven ballots, the Administrator who has served the longest will become the new Coordinator.

The Coordinator will be the presiding officer over all departments of the government.

The term of office for all Administrators will be three years. No Administrator may serve more than three terms in any position.

Amendments
Amendments to this Constitution may be

proposed by The Coordinator, The Executive Committee, The Congress, and by a two-thirds majority vote of the citizens.

Amendments to this Constitution may only be ratified by a two-thirds majority of the Congress in two consecutive congressional terms.

Elections
All elections shall be publicly financed, and only publicly financed. Any donation or gift of any kind with value over $100 to any public official or prospective public official running for office shall be considered attempted bribery. Any attempt to conceal gifts above that limit shall be considered corruption and obstruction of justice, and shall be met with the severest possible consequences, including proportional financial penalties and in extreme cases, the loss of citizenship.

Corporations
Money is property, not speech, and has no right to participate in the political process. Doing so is a felony by the property owner or owners.

Corporations are property and are not entitled to any provisions of personhood.

As property, corporations have no rights under this Constitution, except as defined by law.

Specifically, corporations have no rights except as the property of their owners and/or shareholders. Owners and shareholders shall bear full responsibility for the behavior of the corporation.

Corporations may not participate in politics in any way, not by donation of funding or other resources, not by lobbying, not by the endorsement of specific individuals or any legislative actions, or any other way of influencing the rights of the people to determine their own government. No corporation shall be immune to lawsuits filed against its actions. Should any federal court find that a corporation has exerted inappropriate influence in public or political activities, the Supreme Court shall have the authority to issue appropriate injunctions and penalties upon that corporation, including, but not limited to the immediate revocation of that corporation's charter and its assets held in trust until such time as an appropriate resolution can be determined, where necessary by the joint approval of the Executive Committee and the Congress.

Any crimes committed by any corporation shall be the responsibility of the owners and shareholders of that corporation and they shall be held accountable for the actions of that corporation. They shall be brought before the appropriate agencies of the Department of Justice.

All corporations must be 67% employee owned. All full-time employees shall receive shares of that corporation's stock, equal to their wages, and shall have full voting rights for all shares of stock they own.

ABOUT THE AUTHOR

David Gerrold's work is known around the world. His novels and stories have been translated into more than a dozen languages. His TV scripts are estimated to have been seen by more than a billion viewers.

Gerrold's prolific output includes stage shows, teleplays, film scripts, educational films, computer software, comic books, more than 50 novels and anthologies, and hundreds of articles, columns, and short stories.

He has worked on a dozen different TV series,

including *Star Trek*, *Land of the Lost*, *Twilight Zone*, *Star Trek: The Next Generation*, *Babylon 5*, and *Sliders*. He is the author of *Star Trek*'s most popular episode "The Trouble With Tribbles."

Many of his novels are classics of the science fiction genre, including *The Man Who Folded Himself*, the ultimate time travel story, and *When HARLIE Was One*, considered one of the most thoughtful tales of artificial intelligence ever written. His stunning novels on ecological invasion, *A Matter For Men*, *A Day For Damnation*, *A Rage For Revenge*, and *A Season For Slaughter*, have all been best sellers with a devoted fan following. His young adult series, *The Dingilliad*, traces the healing journey of a troubled family from Earth to a far-flung colony on another world. His *Star Wolf* series of novels about the psychological nature of interstellar war are in development as a television series.

A ten-time Hugo and Nebula award nominee, David Gerrold is also a recipient of the Skylark Award for Excellence in Imaginative Fiction, the Bram Stoker Award for Superior Achievement in Horror, and the Forrest J. Ackerman lifetime achievement award.

In 1995, Gerrold shared the adventure of how he adopted his son in *The Martian Child*, a semi-autobiographical tale of a science fiction writer who adopts a little boy, only to discover he might be a Martian. *The Martian Child* won the science fiction triple crown: the Hugo, the

Nebula, and the Locus. It was the basis for the 2007 film *Martian Child* starring John Cusack and Amanda Peet.

Gerrold's greatest writing strengths are generally acknowledged to be his readable prose, his easy wit, his facility with action, the accuracy of his science, and the passions of his characters. An accomplished lecturer and world traveler, he has made appearances all over the United States, England, Europe, Canada, Australia, and New Zealand. His easy-going manner and disarming humor have made him a perennial favorite with audiences.

David Gerrold is the 2022 winner of the Robert A. Heinlein Award.

BOOKS BY THIS AUTHOR

Praxis

A lifetime in the Labor Corps—or colonize a new world. For Jamie and José, not much of a choice. But Praxis wouldn't be easy. To survive there, you had to depend on each other. And that requires honesty that few possess. Praxis is a bold experiment in society building, a monosexual colony, with no promises of survival and no return trip. But it's got potential. You just have to build a new civilization—on the other side of the universe.

"A wonderfully realized and self-contained story about sexual ambivalence (amongst many other things) that nevertheless leaves you hoping Gerrold's next SF tale picks up where this one leaves off."

—Nigel Suckling, Hugo Award-winning author

"*Praxis* is one of the very few books I've read where the premise of the society/world/universe is so interesting that it engages regardless of the plot. And the plot is a novel and unusual possible human situation, driven by the constraints of what may well come to pass, where traditional space opera is dragged screaming and kicking into a future with brand-new conventions. What *Praxis* is really (as is all the best SF), is the intro for a never-ending epic. But the evocative set-up is what I look for in speculative literature—and this book serves as a magnificent springboard for the reader's imagination."

—F. J. Bergmann, SFPA Grand Master & editor

"The thought-provoking story of two partners set to embark on a one-way trip to a planet that's all men—a literary exploration of human relationships in a brutal society seeking to colonize the universe."

—Dr. Daniel Pomarède, co-discoverer of the Laniakea Supercluster, the South Pole Wall & the Dipole Repeller

"Master of the imagination David Gerrold does it again, *Praxis* is a story of letting go, communication, and acceptance. For men to find a new way they must first redefine manhood, break from an oppressive society, and together learn what it means to become a new type of human."

—Jean-Paul L. Garnier, editor of *Star*Line* & *Simultaneous Times*

The Man Without a Planet

The Man Without a Planet is a science fiction reimagining of the classic tale, *The Man Without a Country*—Redmonde had found his niche in the glitterships of high society, reveling in the opulence and gamesmanship it afforded, until a sudden regime change leads to his permanent exile in the far reaches of space aboard starships building a network of portals through the cosmos. He will never be allowed to see his home world again and escape would seem to be an impossibility—but when the opportunity presents itself, Redmonde disappears into legend.

"In *The Man Without a Planet*, David Gerrold has given us an ambitious reinterpretation of a classic. In this engaging science fiction retelling of *The Man Without a Country*, we find the main character, Redmonde, negotiating the sharp edges of his quarantined banishment in deep space and the intersection of his personal belief system with the sledgehammer of an imposed political ideology."

—Katerina Bruno, science fiction poet and 2022 SFPA Dwarf Stars Award finalist

The Boy Who Was Girl

Whatever you do, don't piss off Slither. That's the only warning you're going to get. Slither is an augmented, shapeshifting assassin with a hair-trigger temper. Hurled across space to a world of violence and treachery, a place where no one can be trusted, Slither can't get home until she (or maybe he?) stops an interplanetary invasion. What happens next is a ferocious, fast-paced brawl where revenge is a dish best served NOW. Fasten your seatbelt! This is David Gerrold at his best!

"A thrilling journey through portals and possibilities, this fast-paced adventure redefines heroism with a gender-fluid protagonist at its heart. With augmented humans, war-loving monocultures, and physical challenges, the story builds into a breakneck speed adventure. David Gerrold has created a classic science fiction tale infused with a fresh, modern perspective."

—Wendy Van Camp, Poet Laureate Emerita & editor of *Eccentric Orbits*

"Travel with Slither, a shapeshifting agent from the future Earth to a world populated by a male monoculture. As the only woman on this world, Slither soon discovers these men are up to no good. A highly recommended read that will keep you turning pages."

—Brian Lebansky, science fiction poet & co-discoverer of a purple acid phosphatase

Praxis II: Praxis Makes Permanent

Praxis Makes Permanent is the highly anticipated conclusion to *Praxis*! Jamie and José have hurtled headlong into a world where nothing is what it's supposed to be. Praxis is in rebellion, but who are the players and what do they want to achieve? If everything is chaotic, where do Jamie and José fit in? And guess what? They're the biggest part of the problem!

"This sequel completely fulfills the promise of the first volume, creating a vision of the future that feels plausible and full of hope, despite that future's gritty, messy imperfection."

—Nigel Suckling, Hugo Award-winning author

"Only David Gerrold could deliver a novella this sharp, this smart, and this deeply human. Gerrold doesn't just write science fiction—

he builds futures with heart, wit, and razor-edged insight. *Praxis Makes Permanent* is bold, unflinching and hard to put down."

—K. Pimpinella, author of the *Time Ranger* series

Available everywhere that great books are sold.

FORTHCOMING BOOKS BY THIS AUTHOR

The Praxis Papers (Praxis I & II)

Thank you for purchasing this book!